"This novel will rank among the best
American racing mysteries."
Thoroughbred Record

"Sherburne does a graceful, understated job
with the swirling Saratoga atmosphere."
The Kirkus Reviews

"A MUST FOR THE MYSTERY FAN."
Indianapolis News

"ENTERTAINING."
Newsday

DEATH'S PALE HORSE

DEATH'S PALE HORSE

A Novel of Murder
in Saratoga in the 1880s

James Sherburne

Based on Research by Betty Borries

FAWCETT GOLD MEDAL • NEW YORK

A Fawcett Gold Medal Book
Published by Ballantine Books
Copyright © 1980 by James Sherburne

Library of Congress Catalog Card Number: 79-26061

ISBN 0-449-13132-7

Manufactured in the United States of America

First Ballantine Books Edition: April 1987

To DAVID
Better late than never

Contents

1

Taking the Waters and Improving the Breed

The first time I saw Kate Linnett on the Piazza of the United States Hotel in Saratoga Springs I felt the thrill of recognition. But whether it was the recognition of a real person unclearly remembered, or of a fantasy created from the dewdrops and moonbeams of my own imagination, I was not sure.

Which is perhaps an overly florid way for a racetrack columnist to begin an account of the sensational and criminal events that occurred at Saratoga last spring. But the point is, I *wasn't* sure whether I had seen her before, or made her up in my dreams. And in this narrative I am determined to tell the literal and exact truth even if it makes me sound like a pre-Raphaelite poet with a flower tucked behind his ear. Or, like the most abandoned sensualist, if it comes to that.

She was unusually tall for a woman, and quite slim except for the high, full breasts that her loose shirtwaist could not hide. Her thick and lustrous brown hair, tinted with auburn, was worn in a pompadour. Full brows arched high over slightly slanted eyes, giving her an expression of half-surprise touched with mockery. Her lips were full, but their softness was partly contradicted by the firm chin below them.

She was pushing an old woman in a wheelchair along the broad colonnaded porch. As I ascended the steps our eyes met, and it seemed her gaze hesitated a moment before passing on, and the slightest suggestion of a frown rippled her placid features. I gave an automatic bob of my head, but her eyes were already beyond me, and she and the old woman continued their way past the wicker rocking chairs that lined the quarter-mile long piazza.

I paused and stared after her, asking myself if I had ever seen her before, and if so, where. But it was no good. I shrugged and entered the hotel.

The great white-tiled lobby was crowded and noisy, and the air was heavy with the mingled scents of Havana cigars and expensive perfume, which half a hundred fluttering fans did nothing to dispel. I threaded my way to the desk and identified myself to the clerk. "Paddy Moretti of *The Spirit of the Times*. I have a reservation."

He inspected me through goiterous eyes. "Oh, have you?" he asked unbelievingly. "We're absolutely full up, you know. We have a waiting list. Some very famous people are on it."

"M-O-R-E-T-T-I. It's an Italian name. The first name is Paddy, which isn't. Look it up in your reservation file."

Frowning, the clerk ran through a pigeonhole-full of reservations and separated one from the others. "Here it is. One single room without bath. On the top floor. At the back, right over the tradesmen's loading dock." His voice gained animation as he continued, "It gets the morning sun from five A.M. on. The bathroom's quite a ways down the hall. Up under the roof there, it gets frightfully hot late in the afternoon." He sounded quite cheerful as he concluded, "It's just about the worst room in the hotel."

"That's fine. Let me sign the book." I wasn't surprised about the room. When my editor, Otto Hochmuth, made a reservation for one of his reporters, it was invariably the least expensive accommodation available. "I enjoy discomfort," I told the clerk. "It keeps me in shape for my adventurous life."

The room was everything he had led me to expect, a cubbyhole the size of a large closet, made to appear even smaller by its oppressive maroon wallpaper. There was barely room to pass between the chiffonier and the bed, and the curtains over the small window were as motionless after the bellboy raised the sash as they were before.

I gave the boy a dime and returned his outraged glare with an expression of cool disdain. When he had left I shed my coat, collar, tie and shirt and stretched out on the bed, hoping for a quick nap to get me through the heat of the afternoon. But sleep was slow in coming, and as the bedsheets dampened under me, my mind moved restlessly over my current situation.

Otto Hochmuth was out to nail my hide to the wall, I was sure of that. It had been written in his bloodshot little eyes every time he looked my way for the past month—ever since I had reported the Governor's presence at the opening of the Monmouth meet on the same day the daily newspapers announced his admission to the hospital for treatment of a bladder infection. It was the kind of mischance that happens to all newspapermen once in a while—or at any rate, to all newspapermen who drink—but Otto Hochmuth took it as evidence of chronic unreliability and a frivolous nature undesirable in a sports columnist of *The Spirit of the Times*. Since then Hochmuth had taken every opportunity to remind me that I was on probation, and that nothing would give him greater pleasure than resolving the uncertainty with my dismissal, *sans* recommendation.

My present assignment was to cover the August meet of

the Saratoga Springs Society for the Improvement of the Breed, two weeks of racing scheduled to reach its climax in a match race between the two greatest horses of the decade, The Mogul and Tenstrike, on the first Saturday of the meet. This match race promised to be the biggest racing event of the year, for it would resolve three bitter public rivalries—that between the horses, who had seesawed between victories in their previous races; between their owners, who had expressed their dislike for one another a number of times; and between their jockeys, the hot-tempered Scot, Jackie McCandless and the coolly professional Negro, Isaac Murphy. As the special correspondent for *The Spirit of the Times,* my account would attract particular attention. It was not an assignment on which I could afford to fail.

After ten minutes on the damp sheets I gave it up. A quick rinse and a brisk toweling left me momentarily dry, and I hurried into fresh linen and a new collar and tie. Three minutes later I was back in the lobby.

The first people I saw there were the tall young woman pushing the wheelchair, and the white-haired old woman sitting in it. This time I had an opportunity to take a careful look at the invalid. She was apparently in her sixties, with a heavily lined face, strong features, and a sunken mouth. Her skin was coated with powder and her cheeks were incongruously bright with rouge. Her dark eyes seemed unfocused as they gazed out from beneath drooping lids. Although the temperature in the hotel lobby must have been in the middle eighties, she was bundled in a crocheted afghan that covered her from her shoulders to her knees.

Once again I bowed as they passed. The old woman took no notice, but her companion glanced at me, her eyebrows rising slightly.

"I beg your pardon, but haven't we met?" I asked, half-embarrassed by the banality of the question.

The tiny twist at the corner of her full lips indicated the impossibility of the idea. "I certainly doubt it," she said. Her voice was a husky alto. They swept past me toward the elevator and disappeared in the crowd. I stared after them until a fat man with mutton-chop whiskers caromed into me, glared furiously, said, "Watch yourself, fellow, damn it!" and pushed hurriedly by. I watched him until he, too, disappeared. Then I shrugged and left the hotel. Outside the temperature seemed to have dropped by a degree or two, but that may have been an illusion.

By the time I reached the stables most of the afternoon's races had been run, and the grounds were bustling with happy winners, dejected losers, and a majority to whom horse racing was a business rarely marked with either emotional extreme. Among this third group was Isaac Murphy.

I had met the famous black jockey a number of times in the past three years, and I liked him very much. When I saw him approaching I waved my arm and shouted, "Hey, Ike. What did you do with that extra twenty pounds?"

He looked puzzled a moment, then grinned as he pinned down the reference. He patted his stomach. "Starved off some of it, and sweated off some, and I reckon the ponies just bounced off the rest." Seeing him at his riding weight of 120 pounds, it was hard to believe he had weighed over 140 in May, but it was true. Murphy always gained twenty pounds over the winter and suffered through their loss in the spring. "How are you, Paddy? Keeping all right?" he asked genially as we shook hands.

"Hanging on by my toenails. What I need right now is some decent copy on your match race this weekend. Otherwise, the days when you can count on having a friend on *The Spirit of the Times* may be numbered."

He looked at me quizzically. "What you been up to now, Paddy?" I told him about my article placing the Governor at Monmouth track during his bladder operation.

Murphy shook his head. "You should have knowed a story like that wouldn't hold water," he said solemnly.

We walked together past the stalls in the main barn and talked about the match race. I was aware of the curious glances we received from some of the grooms and exercise boys, and I knew they were justified in part by our incongruous appearance. Next to Murphy I looked like an unkempt Old English sheepdog beside a champion Doberman pinscher. He always dressed impeccably, in a style which, if not flamboyant, was certainly noticeable. His suit fitted his small, muscular body more tightly than fashion required, and his lavender flowered waistcoat would not have been selected by many members of the Harvard Club. His skin was the color of a new-minted penny, and his features were Caucasian, so that he looked more like a Hindu or an Egyptian than a Negro. He stood just five feet tall, and his legs were short in proportion to his body, but he held himself so erect he seemed two or three inches taller than that. His step was buoyant; as we walked side by side his stride was equal to mine, although I was almost a foot taller, and his pace was brisker than I found comfortable. A few minutes with Murphy made me intensely aware that my suit was wrinkled, my heels were run-down, and my stomach showed an inexorable tendency to bulge over my belt buckle.

He talked about the two horses, The Mogul and Tenstrike. Under most conditions The Mogul was the better horse, he felt. The big gray five-year-old was a superb distance runner who loved to win, responding to his rider's hands and heels with little need of a whip. He was dependable, and had the stamina to hold up through the two-and-a-half-mile distance. Tenstrike, on the other hand, was temperamental. He was capable of astonishing bursts of speed when he felt competitive, but when he didn't, he could slouch around the track like a sullen schoolboy. "It all depends on which side of the stall Tenstrike gets up on," Murphy summarized. "If he gets up feeling lazy, old Mogul should just walk home. But if he gets up feeling his oats, Mogul and I are going to have to hump. I can't tell you anything more than that, Paddy."

"Well, hasn't The Mogul had a better season this year than Tenstrike?" He acknowledged the fact. I pointed out that in his last two races Tenstrike had hardly bothered to run at all. Murphy agreed. "Then I think I'd be pretty confident if I were you," I said.

Murphy was silent a moment. "I suppose so. Only somehow . . . it's as if . . ." His words trailed off, and he chuckled. "Sometimes there just ain't no pleasing a man, is there? No, The Mogul's in fine shape, and we're going to win. You put that in your paper, hear?"

"How about your friend Jackie McCandless? You expect any trouble from him?"

Murphy smiled blandly. "Why, I think you better ask Mr. McCandless that, Paddy. I certainly wouldn't want to put words in his mouth."

Jackie McCandless didn't like Negroes. He especially didn't like Negroes who presumed to enter his profession and beat him at it. Last year he had publicly referred to Isaac Murphy as a "damned black monkey on a stick" and later had struck him with his whip during a race, for which he had been disqualified and suspended for thirty days. Murphy had never made a public comment on the incident, but his private feelings were no secret.

I pressed the question. "What do you think? Do you expect him to ride a clean race?"

Murphy's smile widened, revealing fine white teeth. "I always expect everybody to ride a clean race, and I am hardly every disappointed," he said primly. "Even if Man is born unto trouble, as the sparks fly upward, like the Good Book says."

"You're very pious today, Ike," I said dryly. He lowered his eyes. "How about Harrison Fowler? Has he given you any special instructions?" Fowler was the owner of The Mogul. I had never met him, but by reputation he was egotistical and overbearing.

"Why, he has suggested that I win the race, if that's what you mean."

"Comments like that aren't going to do me much good with Otto Hochmuth." I put my pad and my pencil into my pocket. "Off the record, Ike, give me some idea of what to watch for. Something everybody else isn't going to be concentrating on. Something I can develop over the next couple of days and play up in my match race story. You know what I mean?"

Ike's expression was sympathetic, but he shook his head. "There's nothing I can say, because there's nothing I *know*. It's just a feeling I've got."

"All right, give me the feeling."

"It's—it's the *pressure*. It's pushing down in funny ways. You expect pressure in a big race, especially a grudge race like this. Only this time it's coming stronger from some places where you wouldn't expect it, and not so strong from other places where you would." His forehead creased, and he twisted the wide gold ring on his left ring finger as he attempted to express his feelings accurately. "Mr. Fowler, the Dunne brothers, Jackie McCandless— it's like they're all getting ready for some other race that I don't know about." He snorted in vexation. "Even The Mogul—sometimes even he don't feel like the same horse I rode this spring. Oh, he *is*—I don't mean he's a ringer. But somehow he doesn't exactly *feel* like it. Always used to be we understood each other, he could tell what I wanted him to do without me hardly touching him. But now—well, it's different, that's all."

"What's causing it, Ike?" I asked eagerly, sensing the slant I had hoped for.

He shook his head again. "That's all I can tell you. Because it's just feelings." He hesitated, and when he spoke again his voice was reflective. "There was one time back in the Bluegrass, when I was a boy working for Mr. James T. Williams on his farm near Lexington. I must have been about fourteen. One day there was this same feeling, like things were pushing down on you in different ways. It spooked everybody, even the horses. Things sounded peculiar—noisy things sounded like they were far away, and quiet things, like hay rustling under your boot, they sounded as loud as guns going off. And smells were funny. I never minded manure smell, but that day it caught in my throat like the stink of horse piss, you know?" I nodded.

"Everybody felt it, but nobody knew how come, or who was to blame," he went on somberly. "We watched each other out of the corners of our eyes, and tried to steer clear of each other as much as we could. Couldn't hardly wait till quitting time, so we could get shut of one another."

"Well, did anything really happen?" I asked.

"Oh, yes. Oh, yes indeed. That night a man named Clump, a big, quiet fellow who'd worked for Mr. Williams for years, hard worker, married, two pretty little children, he came back to the main stable and set it afire. Then, while the rest of us was trying to get the horses out alive, he went back to his house and cut his wife and children's throats and blew his brains out with a shotgun."

"Good God Almighty, why?"

Murphy shrugged his shoulder. "Nobody even knew. Some people said he was hoodooed. There was a conjure woman he'd had some trouble with over a milk cow, and she allowed as how she fixed Clump, but I always figures she was just trying to drum up trade. There were other stories—that he had a disease that rotted out his mind, and that he had given it to his family; that he had a grudge against Mr. Williams from when they were both kids—I heard a lot of talk, but nobody ever really knew for a fact what happened. So after a while the talk stopped, and that was that.''

He was silent a moment, and then made an impatient gesture with his hands as if he were a swimmer parting the water in front of him. ''Have you seen The Mogul yet, Paddy?''

''Not since May. I'd like to.''

''Come on, he's just down the line.'' We walked past five stalls, and there he was—a four-legged concentration of grace and speed seventeen hands high, with an iron-gray coat and a white mane and a nose like a Roman senator. I did exactly what I had done the last time I saw him—I gasped. I had never seen another racehorse like him, and to this day I still never have. ''Hey, Big Trouble, look who I brought to see you,'' Ike called. ''It's that man that writes those nice things about you.''

I could have sworn that the big stallion looked at me with recognition, even though I knew it was impossible. I reached my hand into the stall, and he moved toward it, snuffling. ''Hey, Mogul, you remember me. Come here, fellow. Come here and say hello.'' Cautiously he advanced his velvety muzzle into the palm of my hand.

Just then a fist struck my shoulder and a voice shouted in my ear, ''What do you think you're doing with that horse? God-dammit, get away from that stall.''

I spun around to face the same fat man with muttonchop whiskers who had collided with me in the lobby of the United States Hotel an hour before. His face was purple with rage, affording a colorful contrast to his bottle-green suit and silver vest. He drew his fist back, and I raised my hands defensively. ''Now, wait a minute—'' I began.

Ike Murphy interrupted. ''It's all right, Mr. Fowler. This

is Paddy Moretti. He writes articles for *The Spirit of the Times.*"

"I don't give a damn if he's James Gordon Bennett—he's got no business trying to put his hands on The Mogul." He seized my wrists with a surprising grip. "Let's see what you've got in those hands, Mister Writer."

I opened both hand and turned them palm-up. "Look, nothing. I just wanted to pat him. I'm sorry, but there's no damage done."

He glared at me a moment from tiny bloodshot eyes and then released my wrists. He turned to Ike Murphy. "I'm surprised at you, Murphy. You know my rules. No outsiders anywhere near him, and nobody touches him or feeds him but his own stable boys. Christ, is that too much for you to get through that African ivory skull of yours?"

I smiled as ingratiatingly as I could and spoke before the jockey could answer. "If you can forgive me for getting off on the wrong foot, maybe we can start over again, Mr. Fowler." I faked a touch of brogue. "For, to tell you the truth, of all the horsemen in Saratoga, you're the one I want most to interview." *And show up for the ham-haunched boor you are,* I added mentally.

"Want me to help you sell your papers for you? Well, I haven't any time for that now." He deliberately turned his back on me and said to Murphy, "I want to talk to you. Privately."

Murphy's eyes met mine, and he raised one eyebrow slightly, in the equivalent of an apologetic shrug.

I wandered on through the stables and then across to the track, looking for familiar faces. I found one near the paddock, a long-nosed dyspeptic one attached to a tall, skinny body dressed in soiled seersucker. It was a fellow turf reporter named Sharples, who signed his dispatches to *The Thoroughbred Record* with the pen name "Centaur."

Sharples and I had alway gotten on well enough, and he

was willing—for the expected fee of drinks and dinner—to
supply me with background on upcoming races, information which was available to everyone, but would have taken
me hours to assemble. Leaning against the paddock fence,
he fired his facts in telegraphic style as I filled a dozen
pages in my notebook. Then he said abruptly, "This is
thirsty and debilitating work, Moretti. I am failing rapidly."

I closed the notebook and put it away. "All right, where
do you want to go?"

He closed his eyes and smiled a broad anticipatory smile.
"The Club House might be salubrious," he suggested.

"Ah, so it might. We could dine on turtle soup and
woodcock and a beef tournedos, washed down with jere-
boams of vintage champagne and capped with fishbowls of
Napoleon brandy. And then, with body and soul held together for another few hours, perhaps a small outing at the
roulette tables. How does that sound?"

We were walking toward the carriage turnaround, and I
signaled an empty cab. The driver flicked his whip over
his dispirited horse.

Sharples' smile had broadened, and his eyes remained
closed. I helped him into the coach. I told the driver, "Dirty
Helen's."

Sharples' eyes snapped open and his smile disappeared.
"That wasn't nice, Paddy," he said, more in sorrow than
in anger. He slumped down in the coach seat until his chin
almost touched his bony knees.

Dirty Helen's was formally named the Saratoga Chip,
but no one ever called it that. It was the least respectable
of the Springs' seven gaming clubs currently operating—
the number changed every year depending on the state of
the war between the town's churchgoing elders and the
summertime "sportsmen" from New York City who
formed the gambling establishment. An ex-madam named

Helen Liebowitz acted as manager; no one knew who the real owners were. Under her cold eye the club offered questionable food and crooked gambling, but the liquor wasn't watered and the prices were, for Saratoga, low. During the month of August the gentlemen of the fourth estate made it their headquarters. Sharples had probably eaten there at least once a day since he had arrived.

"Look at the bright side," I told him. "By not taking you to the Club House I'm helping you not to form tastes above the capacity of your pocketbook, which could lead you into criminal ways. So don't look a gift horse in the mouth, even if it's on your plate."

We took two seats in the smoky bar, which was already crowded. Sharples ordered a glass of Fish House Punch and I requested an Irish wiskey. Sharples tasted the punch and grimaced.

"What kinds of booze are they getting rid of today?" I asked.

He sucked his teeth analytically. "Apparently rum, Holland gin, very young whisky, and some sort of liqueur that tastes like rotten bananas," he answered. "A festive cup indeed."

We talked and drank for half an hour. After his third Fish House Punch Sharples began to show the effects. We were talking, I think, about the approaching presidential election—Cleveland's bastard child, James G. Blaine waving the "bloody shirt," the Confederate battle flags, all those issues that then seemed so riveting, and now, only a year later, require effort to recollect—when he leaned toward me and said in a stage whisper, "Everybody's a prisoner, that's the point. You, me, Gussie Belmont, Lennie Jerome, goddam Grover Cleveland, everybody! Agreed?"

"All right, agreed. You ready to eat?"

"No, no!" He waved his hand impatiently. "The point is, prisoners can be profitable. It all depends on what kind of a prisoner you are. Or whose." He giggled. "You don't know what the hell I'm talking about, do you?"

"I don't, for a fact."

"How many different kinds of prisoners do you know, Paddy? Prisoners of war? Prisoners of love? Prisoners of the past? Prisoner of Chillon?" He emptied his glass. "You're not even warm. English prisoners? German prisoners? French prisoners? Italian prisoners? Hey, you're getting warmer, Paddy—you're moving in on it, boy."

I answered irritably, "I have no interest in playing guessing games. Or prisoner's base either, for that matter. Do you want another drink, or do you want to eat? Either way is all right with me."

He gave me a look of owlish commiseration. "You're basically an unlucky man. If it was raining diamonds you'd get your hands stuck in your pockets. Your friends all try to help you out, but how far can friends go?" He shook his head sorrowfully. "Since you insist, I'll have another Fish House Punch."

"You do," rasped a hoarse contralto voice at my elbow, "and we'll have to stand you up in the corner like a board." Helen Liebowitz, majestic in crimson moiré and feathers, looked down on us sternly. "Don't you know that three's the limit on Fish House, even for boys who can hold their liquor?" She turned her head and shouted to the headwaiter standing in the door to the dining room, "Hey, Etienne, a table for two for these bozos."

Sharples grinned at her foolishly. "Hello, Helen. Why don't you buy us a round and tell us about prisoners? Come on—there's not much you miss around here. You know what I'm talking about even if old Paddy doesn't."

Helen Liebowitz narrowed her painted eyes and frowned. Then she smiled broadly, and a gold bicuspid caught the light. "Slats, you've got more you-know-what than a Christmas turkey. But I'm shutting off your water right now, so you might as well go in there and eat your supper. Hell, if you don't get some food in you, how are you going to be in condition to lose money at the tables?''

It seemed to me she was talking in an unusually loud voice until I realized that most of the other people in the bar had fallen silent. Glancing around the room I looked into half a hundred pairs of curious eyes. I felt suddenly embarrassed. "I think she has a point, Sharples. What would you say to a T-bone, medium rare . . .''

Sharples let out a bray of laughter and slapped the mahogany bar. "*Medium* rare—medium! Ah, you're sharp as a razor.'' His shoulders shook.

I put my hand under his elbow and drew him away from the bar. Dirty Helen's eyes met mine. I noticed she was wearing a black beauty patch below her left ear. The skin around it was coarse-pored and caked with powder. "Suppertime!'' I said cheerfully. "Try to force yourself. Remembering that I'm paying.''

Sharples followed me into the dining room. We ordered steaks and waited for them to be served. I tried to keep the conversation lively, but found I was conducting a monologue; for some reason Sharples had sunk into a moody silence. He sat slumped in his chair, his bony jaw on his chest, studying his interlaced fingers on the table before him. Every so often he would raise his eyes to mine, and an expression of sullen withdrawal would cross his face. After a few minutes I grew tired of it.

"I don't know what's eating you, but whatever it is, I've had about enough. When somebody's buying your supper, the least you can do is make a little pleasant conversation.''

He grinned crookedly. "You think a piece of beefsteak gives you the right to pick over my brain like a ragman in a junkyard? Well, think again. Oh, I know what you're after, Moretti. I could see you working up to it ever since you tied on to me in the paddock. Worming your way into my confidence—trying to get me drunk on Fish House Punch—talking about things you have no business knowing about . . ." He shook his head. "You're like all the rest of 'em, just looking out for Number One."

Our dinners arrived, giving me an excuse not to reply. We ate in silence. The conversation at the surrounding tables was noisy, which took some of the awkwardness out of it. Halfway through my steak, Helen Liebowitz came by again. Her heavy features were set in a smile but her eyes were careful. "How's the steak, boys?" she asked. Sharples grunted; I said mine was excellent. "Well, eat hearty and give the house a good name." She hesitated as if she were going to say something else then apparently decided against it and moved on to another table.

Sharples continued to remain silent, but now apparently more because he was sleepy than because of my prying ways. He toyed with his dessert and refused coffee. I paid the check and rose, leaving him nodding in his chair. I said good night as impersonally as I could, and left immediately. On what Otto Hochmuth paid me I couldn't afford to stay and try my luck at the tables.

Dirty Helen's was a few doors off Broadway, and only a few hundred yards from the United States Hotel. My route took me along the edge of Congress Spring Park. It was still daylight, and the pathways leading to the pavilion were crowded with strollers bent on taking the famous waters. I paused for a moment to watch them, wondering if the warm, salty, mildly effervescent liquid that bubbled up through the rocks had any medicinal value whatever, barring its sometimes surprisingly rapid cathartic effect.

August dusk in Saratoga Springs is the time when one becomes convinced against one's better judgment that the day has been worthwhile. In the shadowy light beneath the great elms the ladies seem younger, more graceful, more finely drawn. The gentlemen take on aspects of seriousness or wit not noticeable during the afternoon. Music from a band concert floats on the air, and rich equipages—coaches, carriages, barouches, phaetons, landaus and victories—pass jingling and whip-snapping in the street. Even to be a spectator is to feel one's own importance.

As I watched the promenaders moving like dancers in a stately and complex figure, I thought *You've come a long way from the trotting track at the Corbo Country Fair Grounds in Goshen, Ohio, Paddy Moretti.* Then, remembering Otto Hochmuth's grim smile, I added, *Now that you're here, try to stay awhile.*

My hotel room had cooled off, and I wrote my first special dispatch to *The Spirit of the Times* in relative comfort. I tried to suggest some of the pressure Isaac Murphy had mentioned, but without any facts it was uphill work. After an hour I read over what I had written without satisfaction. It was acceptable for background—barely acceptable—but I would have to do a good deal better tomorrow if I were to hold my editor at bay. Slipping on my jacket, I started for the telegraph office.

Passing through the lobby, I looked in vain for a beautiful young woman pushing an invalid chair.

I filed my dispatch, returned to the hotel and enjoyed the evening for a few minutes on the piazza, with several hundred other guests. Then I went up to my room, poured myself a nightcap from my flask, and went to bed.

It must have been at just that same time that the first murder was committed.

2
Unusual Contents
of a Dumbwaiter

I dreamed I was back at the trotting track in southern Ohio. It was the summer after I graduated from Goshen High School and I had gotten the job I had prayed for. I was working twelve hours a day, six days a week, as a stable boy.

I had been a fool about horses ever since I could remember. My father, Domenic Moretti, blamed it on my mother's Gaelic blood, and my mother, Sheila (O'Kelly) Moretti, blamed it on the godless Protestants we lived among. Nobody could understand why I played hookey from school or stole away from my father's store when I was supposed to be working, incurring the certainty of a whipping, merely to spend a few hours gawking at racehorses. I couldn't understand it myself; all I knew was that the world held no sharper beauty or more heart-stopping thrills than I found at the track.

In my dream I was in a stall. A horse was lying on its side in the straw, eyes bulging and lips pulled back. It breathed in shuddering gasps, and its hoofs kicked ineffectually against the sod floor. I saw that it was a filly, a small

graceful chestnut with three white stockings. The certainty
filled me that the horse was dying, and that only I could
save her.

I lay down beside her with my arms around her salt-
encrusted neck and my cheek pressed against her nose. Her
body heat struck me like a blast of air from an open fur-
nace. *You're going to be all right, I promise, you're going
to be all right,* I thought or perhaps said aloud. I knew I
was making a solemn commitment, one that entailed obligations I would have preferred to avoid, but I had no
choice. *Believe me, trust me, you're going to be all right.*

The scene changed. Clad in racing silks and boots, I was
sitting on the chestnut filly, poised for the beginning of a
race. (I was quite aware that there were only sulky races
at the Goshen track, but this made no difference to the
dream-logic of the experience.) Other horses were lined up
to the right and left, and other riders, visible only in profile, leaned purposefully forward. With a sudden roar the
race began.

As we moved toward the first turn I realized a number
of things simultaneously. One was that the chestnut had
the ability to win, but she couldn't do it by herself; she
was dependent on my help. Another was that, although the
prize for winning the race was modest, the price of losing
would be disastrous. A third was that I was in grave moral
and physical danger.

At the first pole the horses began to string out. We were
in the middle of the string. The horse behind was falling
back, and I began to close on the sorrel ahead. The chestnut filly was running so smoothly it seemed effortless, yet
I knew every muscle was stretched to the utmost. We
moved even with the sorrel, then passed it and began to
overtake the next one in the string. By the time we came
out of the last turn and entered the stretch we were in
second place, trailing the front runner by less than two

lengths. Then the chestnut somehow found the extra speed to move up, and suddenly we were neck and neck pounding toward the wire. The grandstand was on my right, and I was dimly aware of the shouting crowd, all waving arms and open mouths.

Then, not fifty yards from the finish, I saw *her*. She was dressed as she had been in the hotel lobby, a loose white shirtwaist with a man's tie knotted at the collar, and a full skirt of stiff taffeta in a tartan pattern. Her breasts swelled beneath the blouse, and her full red lips turned down at one corner. She stood coolly beside the guardrail, shielding herself from the sun with a frilly parasol, an island of calm in a sea of excitement.

Our eyes met, and I felt that suddenly half my purpose was drained away. The pounding of hoofs in my ears receded. The muscles in my arms, thighs and calves felt strained and awkward, demanding easement. *What am I doing here?* I asked myself. *I shouldn't be here. I should be there, with her.*

Then, as clearly as any spoken word, I heard the mind of the chestnut filly crying to me. *But you promised! You promised I was going to be all right!* And at that moment she broke down and began to fall. Her front legs crumpled under her and her head struck the dirt. Her momentum carried her over in a cartwheel. When her back struck the ground one of my legs was under it.

For a moment pinned beneath the weight of the broken horse, my eyes met *hers* again. She smiled with humorous commiseration, as at one of life's little irritations. That smile was the last thing I saw before the sharp hoofs of the horse behind descended on my head and body . . .

I awoke, shaken and filled with feelings of guilt and shame. I was wrapped like a mummy in my damp bed-sheets. The air in the tiny room was hot, humid and utterly still. The gray light of false dawn outlined the window sash, and from the loading platform three floors below I could hear the bang and rattle of the first of the morning's deliveries.

Unable to get back to sleep, I lay spread-eagled on my back and tried to make heads or tails of the dream. From somewhere inside the hotel I heard the whine of a pulley and the thud of a closing door. Footsteps moved along the hall toward the bathroom. Someone in the next room caused his bed to squeak. Each sound came as a separate and distinct irritation. When the sky outside the windows lightened to a pearly iridescence, I gave a sigh of relief and lowered my feet to the floor, glad to give up the unequal struggle and dress for breakfast at the track.

Crossing the hotel lobby toward the piazza I noticed an unusual swirl of activity around the entrance to the dining room. Although it was too early for breakfast in the hotel, a good many hotel employees and guests seemed to have business beyond the elaborately carved doors. (I assumed that the proper-looking men in suits and ties were guests, since I had had little experience with resort policemen in plain clothes.) I gave them no thought.

Breakfast at the track had been a Saratoga institution since the 1870s, when a group of Southern owners who got up early to watch workouts decided to save themselves the trip back to the Springs by breakfasting with their grooms and exercise boys. Their belles soon decided that eating at the stables was *chic,* since that was where the eligible males were; by now what had begun as simple meals had become sumptuous repasts. I enjoyed them because they were relatively inexpensive for the amount of food served, and because they offered the opportunity to talk to a maximum number of racing people in a minimum time.

The tables were set up under a grove of trees between the stables and the paddock. When I arrived there were three or four hundred breakfasters already in attendance—

dapper sportsmen; spoiled rich men's sons, gamblers disguised as gentlemen, magnolia blossoms from Mobile and prickly pears from Austin, touts and jockeys and grooms, early-rising pimps and late-retiring whores, newspapermen who looked like crooks and crooks who looked like deacons. I spied Sharples waiting in line for fried chicken, and joined him.

"Good morning," I said.

"God damn Dirty Helen and her Fish House Punch, and God damn you too, Moretti." He took a breast and moved along to get his hominy grits. I accepted a thigh. By the time we reached the end of the serving line he had added a grilled lamb kidney, two rashers of bacon, a thick slice of beefsteak, corn bread and butter and currant preserves to his plate, which he held in his left hand. His right hand managed a quarter of a honeydew melon balanced on a cup of coffee.

I followed him with a considerably lighter load, and set my plate beside his at a trestle table. I congratulated him on his appetite, and he cursed me again without malice. He ate with steady voracity. I took a bite of chicken and asked, "Do you know anything about a tall girl with reddish-brown hair who pushes an old lady in an invalid chair around the United States Hotel?"

He stopped eating and looked at me. "Why?"

"I think I'm in love with her."

"Like hell. Oh, like hell you are!" He glared bitterly over a forkful of kidney. "So you *are* onto it. You disgusting mixed-breed liar! And last night butter wouldn't melt in your mouth!"

"Well, whether I am or not, I need some help from you, friend. You know I've never been able to dig out facts like you can. And everybody knows your sources are the best in the business." I went on in this vein until he began to nod his agreement to each new piece of flattery. Then I asked him for his information.

He put his fork down and folded his hands over his stomach. "The old woman's name is Agnes Murchison. She's crippled or paralyzed or something. She comes from somewhere on the Gulf Coast, and she's here to take the waters. A respectable old widow in somewhat strained circumstances. Totally uninteresting, except that she's also a medium."

"You mean in the spiritualist sense? She has séances?"

"As if you didn't know! Yes, she has séances. Attended, so I understand, by some of the richest old dragons in Saratoga. She puts them in contact with defunct relatives and lost loves, for which they are properly grateful. All very hush-hush, of course, but you can't keep anything like that quiet for long. As I'm sure you'll be the first to agree." He grinned mockingly.

"Who's the girl?"

"Kate something—Linley, Linnett, something like that. Paid companion, probably knows nursing, and helps at the séances. No doubt a grade-A student charlatan. But a damned handsome woman, I'll give you that."

I opened my mouth for another question, but he silenced me with a raised hand. "Uh-uh. It's your turn now. What have you heard about them? And where did you hear it? You just got into town yesterday."

I denied any prior knowledge of the two women and their activities. Sharples didn't believe me. "Damn you, Moretti, I told you what I know, now 'fess up. What have *you* got?"

"Nothing but a bad case of unrequited love." I rose from the bench and began looking for familiar faces. "And now, if you'll excuse me—"

Sharples leaned toward me and whispered harshly, "And what about the Prisoner?"

"What prisoner? One of those prisoners you were bab-bling about last night? I don't know what you're talking about." I saw a trainer I knew and moved to join him. I heard Sharples' angry voice behind me: "Moretti, you bas-tard, hold out on me and you'll be sorry."

I moved through the breakfast crowd, asking questions, making notes and sniffing for news. The black jockey, Isaac Murphy, was there, sartorially elegant in a yachting cap, navy blazer and snowy white flannels; we exchanged plea-santries, but he had no news for me. Harrison Fowler, stuffing food into his mouth with mechanical gluttony, didn't deign to acknowledge my presence. I had even worse luck with his competitors.

The Dunne brothers and their jockey, Jackie McCand-less, were standing at the edge of the crowd, talking or perhaps arguing. I knew them all by sight, and didn't hes-itate to join them. "Moretti of *The Spirit of the Times*," I interrupted. "How did Tenstrike do on his workout this morning?"

The three men reacted with varying degrees of irritation. The older Dunne, Fergus, was the least upset. The expres-sion on his long-nosed, clerkish face suggested resignation more than anger—as though life had once again intruded where it had no business to intrude. His watery eyes re-garded me with mild dislike. His brother Tom was ob-viously angry at the interruption. His broad Irish face flushed, his wide shoulders hunched, and he opened his mouth to express himself vigorously. The wiry little man beside him gave him no chance.

"What the hell do you think you're doing, sneaking around where you're not wanted, breaking in on private conversations?" Jackie McCandless yelled. "Clear out of here, you damned snooper!" In contrast to Tom Dunne, he turned white when he was angry; his foxy face, with its colorless hair, eyebrows and lashes, looked like that of an albino. Fists clenched, he took a step toward me. Fergus Dunne put a restraining hand on his shoulder. "No, no, Jackie—don't give way to wrath and violence, whatever the provocation." He looked at me sorrowfully. "Gentlemen wait to be invited before joining private conversations, Mr.—ah, Moretti."

"How the hell would he know about what gentlemen do?" asked Tom. Jackie McCandless sneered in agreement.

"I'm sorry. I didn't eavesdrop, and I'm sorry if I butted in. I just thought you might have a comment for the press on how Tenstrike's shaping up for the match race." I spoke in a conciliatory tone. "Anything you care to say—"

Fergus Dunne smiled gently. "Anything we care to say, we *will* say—in our own good time. You may rest assured of that. And now, if you'll excuse us, Mr. Moretti—"

"Now wait a minute, Mr. Dunne. I don't understand this. Most owners are glad to get all the publicity they can in *The Spirit of the Times*. You people and Harrison Fowler bite my head off if I even ask you a question. What's going on here, anyway?"

McCandless made another move toward me, and Fergus Dunne's hand restrained him again. "Perhaps it has something to do with your approach to your work, young man. Now I suggest you leave us at once. Otherwise I will be forced to lodge a complaint against you with the stewards."

I looked from one to another in frustration. "If you ever decide you want to talk to me, I'll try to be more cooperative than you've been. Good day, gentlemen." I turned away and walked through the thinning crowd of breakfasters to the carriage turnaround.

It was nearly eight-thirty when I returned to the United States Hotel. As I bought a New York City newspaper at the stationery counter, I became aware of a conversation near me. Two matrons were talking animatedly.

". . . and they say he had no clothes on at all! Absolutely naked, if you can imagine that!" said one, whose ostrich plumes bobbed in time with her words. "In the United States Hotel? Well, I declare!" said the other, fluttering her fan in agitation. "That's right—naked as a newborn babe, with his brains beaten out, and wedged into the dumbwaiter like a cork in a bottle!" continued ostrich plumes. "Oh, my dear," cried fluttering fan, "I'll never eat another bit of room service food here as long as I live!"

"Excuse me, ladies," I interrupted, "but do I understand that a man has been found murdered here in the hotel?"

Ostrich plumes included me eagerly in the conversation. Indeed a man had been found murdered, she rattled on. His body had been discovered in the kitchen at six by cooks preparing breakfast. He had been beaten to death, and his corpse—she lowered her eyes briefly—which was totally unclothed, was crammed into a dumbwaiter. The police had arrived and now were questioning the hotel staff. And didn't I agree that such goings-on were a disgrace, and were the result of the lowered moral tone of the nation, due to the deplorable standards set by That Man in the White House?

"There's no doubt about it," I agreed gravely. "Things like this could never happen under James G. Blaine." I bowed and excused myself, and began looking for the police officer in charge of the investigation.

I found him an hour later, at his desk in the annex of City Hall. He was a rough-cut New York State German named Captain Fred Winklemann. He had a square, freckled face, a shock of white hair and small suspicious blue eyes set in a bit too close together.

"No, we don't know who he is," he said in answer to

my question. "So far, all we know is he probably wasn't a guest of the hotel. At least, nobody fitting his description seems to be missing. Why do you care? I thought you worked for a sports newspaper."

I explained that during racing season anything that happened in Saratoga might become sports news. "And if there is some racing connection, Captain, *The Spirit of the Times* just might be the paper to hook it up."

He grunted skeptically. "I'll tell you what I told the other newspapermen, Moretti. I don't want any fancy stories on this. I don't want to see any headlines about Mystery Man Murdered in Saratoga Springs. Understand? Nothing about naked bodies in kitchen dumbwaiters. Nothing about people getting their heads bashed in at the United States Hotel. Nothing that would make the timidest church mouse in the world hesitate one half-second from coming here and spending his money." He leaned back and cracked the knuckles of his large square hands. It was a cautionary sound. "I want to be sure we understand each other about that."

"Captain, believe me, we wouldn't do a thing to embarrass the city or the hotel people—or you either, of course. We're all on the same side, after all—we're all interested in promoting the popularity of horse racing." I made my voice so sincere that for a moment I was afraid I was overdoing it.

He looked at me expressionlessly and then rose abruptly from his chair. "All right, I suppose you want to look at the body. The other reporters saw him, so I guess you can too."

Concealing my surprise at the offer, I followed him down the stairs to the basement. He pushed open a door marked "Morgue" and we entered a bleak room smelling of disinfectant that almost, but not quite, concealed an abiding odor of decomposition. The body lay on a metal table under a stiffly starched sheet. Chief Winklemann flicked the sheet back from the head and torso with a gesture that was almost contemptuous, as though in his experience people who succumbed to death were weaklings or worse. I leaned forward to study the face.

It was the face of a man in his late twenties or early thirties, and he had been handsome when he was alive. His hair was blue-black and curly, except where it was matted with dried blood. His eyes, wide and staring, were the color or ripe olives, and his teeth were even and white. Against the bloodless gray of his skin, the bruises of his forehead and left cheekbone stood out lividly. The death wound was high above his left ear. It was an indentation two inches across and an inch deep, at the bottom of which fragments of white bone gleamed through clotted blood and hair.

As I stared at the corpse's face I had the sensation of partial familiarity—not as if I had known *him* before, but rather a relative of his, a brother perhaps, whose features might have been unlike those of the man on the slab, and yet whose consanguinity with him was apparent.

Winklemann was watching me shrewdly. "Do you know him?" he asked.

I shook my head slowly. "Never saw him before in my life."

Winklemann looked back at the dead face. "He was a vain son-of-a-bitch, whoever he was," he said musingly.

"What makes you say that, Chief?"

"Look where he shaved. No just his chin and upper lip, where you'd expect, but here, between his eyebrows, too." His blunt finger pointed to the space directly above the bridge of the corpse's nose. Looking closely, I saw an almost invisible blue-black stubble.

"I guess you can't blame him," I said. "If he hadn't shaved there, his eyebrows would have run together like a chimpanzee's. Which I don't suppose most ladies would consider a particularly attractive feature. And the consideration of most ladies would be pretty important to him, wouldn't you say?'' Winklemann nodded. ''You think he was in some bed where he didn't belong, and the husband came home early?'' I asked.

''It would explain why he was bare-ass naked.''

''Is there any way to tell which floor of the hotel the body came from? That would narrow things down considerably—I can't see a murderer carrying a naked cadaver up or down a flight of stairs if he doesn't need to.''

Winklemann shook his head. ''There's no way. All we know is that the dumbwaiter was sent down into the kitchen from one of the upper floors.''

We looked at the still body a moment in silence. Winklemann pinched his right ear lobe and I pulled on the end of my nose. I asked, ''Any way to tell what he was hit with?''

The Chief shrugged. ''The usual blunt instrument. At least an inch wide, heavy, with no sharp edges. Beyond that, it could be anything.''

There didn't seem to be anything more to be learned here. I said, ''Well, much obliged, Chief—'' and he pulled the sheet up over the cold face again. We walked back to his office, where I thanked him for his time. He waved my thanks away and fixed me with his hard little eyes.

''I meant what I said, Moretti. I don't like headlines, not about Saratoga. I don't want to be surprised by any. If you find anything that helps hook up that connection you were talking about, you bring it here to this office first— then we'll decide whether or not it goes to your paper.''

''Now, wait a minute, Chief—''

''No, *you* wait a minute. This is my town, and I make the rules. You forget it, and I'll have you barred from the track in five minutes flat, and you won't be able to find a hotel room closer than Albany. Have you got that?'' We looked at each other. His expression allowed no room for negotiation. I nodded. He relaxed slightly and reached out to shake hands without bothering to rise. "O.K., Moretti, nice meeting you," he said in dismissal.

"If you get an identification, will you let me know?"

"Sure. Just ask me."

I walked back to the hotel slowly, turning over the happenings of the past twenty-four hours in my mind. Did they add up to anything? I had no idea. Passing Congress Spring Park I decided to treat myself to a glass of mineral water on the off chance it would clear my brain. I gave one of the dipper-boys a penny and he filled a glass and handed it to me. It tasted just as I remembered it—fizzy, metallic and slightly putrid. I forced myself to finish the glass, thinking *Anything that tastes so awful is bound to be good for you.*

At the desk the clerk with the goiterous eyes handed me my key and a flimsy yellow envelope. Without opening it, I knew it was from Otto Hochmuth. I went to my room and mixed myself a drink from my flask, and then sat on the bed and read the telegram:

PADDY MORETTI, UNITED STATES HOTEL, SARATOGA SPRINGS, N.Y.

LAST STORY UNACCEPTABLE STOP YOU COULD HAVE WRITTEN IT IN TERRE HAUTE INDIANA STOP AM PAYING YOU TO SEND IN MORE THAN LAUNDRY LISTS STOP SUGGEST YOU DECIDE IF YOU ARE MEANT FOR NEWSPAPER WORK STOP THE GOVERNOR OF NEW JERSEY SENDS REGARDS

                                        HOCHMUTH

I drained my glass and mixed another. I began to curse Otto Hochmuth in Italian, in words and phrases I had learned from my Uncle Giovanni. When I ran out of Italian, I switched to the Gaelic vocabulary taught me by my Uncle Seamus.

The telegram enraged me, but did not surprise me. I knew as well as my editor that my first Saratoga story was light on facts and colorless in style. I had played into the hands of my enemy, and had myself to blame. His telegram would have been much easier to bear if I could have told myself it was unwarranted, but I couldn't. All I could do was rage.

I had two more drinks from my flask before I realized it must be afternoon; if I wanted to be at the track for the first race, it was time to leave. I debated whether or not to bother. *What good will it do? He'll get you sooner or later anyway,* I told myself. *But why make it easier for him?* I argued. *On the other hand, you could make it easier on yourself—just stay here and get drunk. But who says you can't have a few drinks at the track while you're working?*

The upshot of the debate was that I had another drink and went to the track.

I moved through the afternoon in a haze of industriousness, anger and self-pity, sustaining my level of intoxication with additional infusions after the second and fourth races. Oddly enough, I worked very well. My notes were copious, and contained a number of exclusive facts and observations. If Hochmuth were to fire me, it wouldn't be on the basis of this day's story, I told myself.

I was at the betting ring, the open shed near the finish line where the bookmakers occupied their individual stalls and quoted their individual odds, when I saw Gus Gibbons. He was talking earnestly to a well-dressed gentleman in a hacking jacket and knickerbockers, clutching the gentleman's elbow with sausage-shaped fingers. Every time he opened his mouth his tiny chin disappeared into his fat neck.

I stepped up to the potential victim. "Pardon me, sir, but I hope you don't plan to invest in any tips this man may offer you. He's been warned off half the tracks in the United States."

The gentleman in the knickerbockers stared first at me, then at Gibbons. "Certainly not! Wouldn't think of it!" he cried in agitation as he turned and disappeared in the crowd.

Gibbons watched his back as long as it was visible, then turned to face me. He was in control of his features, and the hatred that glittered in his eyes was almost perfectly concealed behind an expression of patient martyrdom. "Ah, Paddy—every time I see you I have to turn the other cheek. Even a good Christian like me has to wonder if there's ever to be an end to it."

I grinned at him. "Why, sure—when you've been warned off all the other tracks in the country. The way you're going, that shouldn't take more than another year or two." I jotted down a note on my pad. "How about this for my column tomorrow? 'The flood of touts and petty criminals at Saratoga this season, as typified by the unsavory Gus Gibbons, a convicted thief and pander, should cause concern to all friends of the Sport.' That has a nice ring to it, don't you think?"

Gibbons ran his tongue over his lips before he answered. "You got no reason to write things like that about me," he said huskily.

"No reason but Marya Reznik. Do you ever hear from Marya, or do they let her write letters, wherever she is?"

The hatred in his eyes shone brightly, but his expression became even more hangdog. "Are you going to hold that against me forever? Maybe I made a mistake—I admit it. But I was only trying to help."

"Of course you were. And that's what I'm doing for you. Helping. I'm giving you free publicity. Good day, Mr. Gibbons." I started to turn away from him, but his fat hand caught me by the arm. The mask was gone; his mouth twisted viciously and his fingers bit into my biceps with surprising force.

"You keep after me, and they'll pick you up in a basket, a piece at a time," he whispered with his face an inch from mine. His breath was hot and his spittle sprayed my cheek. "A piece at a time—I promise you, Moretti."

I tore my arm from his grip and walked away from him toward the paddock. I discovered my heart was pounding. Gibbons' final words had affected me more than I wanted to admit.

Our bad blood dated from two years before, when we had both lived in the same boarding house in Chicago for a few weeks. Marya Reznik lived there, too. She was a dark girl with big eyes, a slender neck and a small but beautifully proportioned body. She worked on a machine in one of the second-floor shirtwaist factories on Wells Street. I didn't know her well, because her manner was shy, and she stayed in her own room most of the time.

Then she became ill and lost her job. By the time she was back on her feet her rent was three weeks overdue. She didn't know where to go for money, and Gibbons helped her out. She reimbursed him the only way she could. After a while he persuaded her to accommodate his so-called friends as well. When the landlady kicked her out of her room, Gibbons put her into a house in the First Ward, and her professionalization was complete.

It was a dull and commonplace story, and I don't know why it affected me as strongly as it did. Perhaps because of the quiet modesty of the girl—perhaps because of the lip-smacking description he gave after he became her pimp. At any rate I let him know I despised him. He laughed at me.

A year later I happened to see Marya in a blind tiger on South Wabash Street. Her hair was stringy, her skin blotchy, and her rouge was as garish as a clown's. I started to speak to her, but she pretended not to see me, and left soon afterward. It was then I decided to hurt Gus Gibbons the most effective way I could. I went to the stewards of the Chicago tracks and lodged complaints against him, hinting that if he wasn't barred I would mention it in my column. He was barred. Later, when our paths crossed in Baltimore, I did the same thing at Pimlico.

Today was the first time he had threatened me. That meant our relationship was on a new footing—one that deserved to be thought over very carefully.

The last race ended, and I took my notes back to my room, stopping on the way to pick up a quart of whiskey. I took off my jacket, collar and tie, and began to write my column. At first it went very well; I wrote confidently and treated myself to a short drink every two paragraphs or so. Then gradually apprehensions began to arise. Maybe it wasn't as good as I thought it was—or maybe Otto Hochmuth wouldn't think it was, which for all practical purposes was the same thing. The account of the day's races was certainly adequate, but what about the bigger story, the coming match race? I had nothing new on it at all. How would Hochmuth feel about that? Would it give him the ammunition he needed to shoot me out of the tree?

I had another drink and finished my report. Rivulets of sweat were running into my eyes as I wrote 30 under the final sentence. The confidence with which I had started was as one with the snows of yesteryear. The pencil in my hand was shaking. *What can I do?* I asked myself. *How can I buy more time?*

Suddenly the idea came to me. My editor might be a sour, penny-pinching, unappreciative wretch, but he was also a newspaperman. I hesitated a moment to get my thoughts in order, then began writing again:

PERSONAL TO HOCHMUTH STOP AM FOLLOWING
BREAKING STORY INVOLVING MURDER OF UNIDENTI-
FIED MAN WHOSE NAKED BODY WAS FOUND TODAY
IN UNITED STATES HOTEL STOP POSSIBLE CONNEC-
TION MOGUL TENSTRIKE MATCH RACE STOP NOTO-
RIOUS UNDERWORLD FIGURES MAY BE INVOLVED STOP

I bit the end of my pencil and read over what I had written.
Good, good, I thought, *but it can be better.* I continued:

ALSO EVIDENCE OF SWINDLERS WORKING BIZARRE
CONFIDENCE GAME ON TOP SOCIETY LEADERS STOP
EXPECT TO UNCOVER ALL FACTS WITHIN DAYS STOP
REGARDS

MORETTI

If he can fire me after he reads that, he's not the ink-stained peeping Tom I think he is!

Buoyed by a feeling of self-confidence bordering on euphoria, I took my copy to the telegraph office for transmission to New York. That night I slept like a baby.

3

Crucifixion of a Columnist

The Spirit of the Times is a weekly, but its deadlines are as tight as most metropolitan dailies. My story had gone in only an hour before deadline, so I didn't have long to wait to see it in print.

I awoke too late to eat breakfast at the track, and with a queasiness in the pit of my stomach and a pounding in my temples that would have argued against it even if the hour had allowed it. My tiny room was bright with the morning sun. The rope that was provided as a fire escape lay neatly coiled beneath the window; dust motes danced in the air before settling gently on the heavy black walnut furniture. From outside came the comfortable bustling sounds of a Saratoga morning. They did nothing to dispel my feeling of uneasiness.

I breakfasted in the hotel dining room, that great hall with seats for a thousand simultaneous gourmands, in company with a handful of other late risers. I caught a glimpse of Harrison Fowler leaving as I entered. He looked as though his disposition was worse than it had been the day before.

I took a seat at an empty table for twenty. Although I was as conspicuous as a frog in a bathtub, it took my waiter two minutes to notice my presence. Then he strolled to the table with sedate dignity and halted beside my chair. "Good morning, sah," he said, staring at something six inches above my head. "May I recommend the *crêpes à la maison,* stuffed with crab meat and served with sauce mornay? And would the gentleman take champagne? Might I suggest—"

"I might just possibly get down a soft-boiled egg and a piece of toast," I interrupted hastily. "And a pot of black coffee. *Tout de suite, s'il vous plaît.*"

My accent seemed to cause him physical pain. Watching him as he walked to the kitchen, I reflected on the legendary arrogance of the hotel waiters of Saratoga. Once, according to tradition, a patron anxious to impress his guests had slipped his waiter a ten-dollar bill and whispered, "Just so you'll remember to take good care of us." Half an hour passed, and the waiter failed to return. Excusing himself from his guests, the patron sought him out. "Didn't I give you ten dollars to take good care of my party?" he demanded angrily. The waiter nodded. "If you were going to treat me like this, why did you take my money?" Raising one eyebrow, the waiter answered, "I took it to show you I couldn't be bribed."

My egg arrived in a reasonable time, however, even though it was served with silent disapproval. Anchored with toast and washed down with hot black coffee, it seemed likely to stay where it belonged. My queasiness vanished and my headache abated as I sipped my second cup. I decided I had no cause for uneasiness. I congratulated myself for having handled a difficult situation well. *Paddy, me boyo,* I told myself fatuously, it's a good night's work you did on that spalpeen Hochmuth, for a fact.

After breakfast I walked over to Chief Winklemann's

office. The Chief was busy. A reporter I knew from the New York *Herald* was playing solitaire at a desk outside his closed door. We exchanged greetings, and he expressed surprise at my presence in the police station. "When you work for a sports paper I thought you only came here as an unwilling guest," he said.

I told him that sometimes the fresh open air, the high excitement and the short, easy hours palled on me. "Then I get an urge to return briefly to the squalid scenes of my past," I explained. "Do you know if they've identified the body they found in the dumbwaiter yesterday?"

"If they have, they're keeping it quiet. All Winklemann will say is that the police are following a number of promising leads, et cetera. Who do you like in the match race?"

I told him I liked The Mogul, but I wasn't sure I liked him enough to put up five dollars to win two, which was what the bookmakers were asking. Tenstrike's odds of 2 to 1 were considerably more attractive, but what's the advantage of good odds if the bet doesn't pay off?

"It's all a mug's game anyway," the *Herald* man said, peeking under two piles of cards before making a play on one of them. "Put your money in something sensible, like whiskey or women."

I walked back to the hotel to wait for the New York newspapers to arrive; today, *The Spirit of the Times* would be with them. To pass the time, I jotted down all the famous or notorious people I observed in the lobby during a twenty-minute period, planning to salt my next column with their names. My notes tell me that I saw Diamond Jim Brady, glittering like a crystal chandelier as he promenaded arm in arm with the amply rounded Lillian Russell; William Henry Vanderbilt in his yachting costume and Jay Gould dressed like a shabby Presbyterian clergyman from a Highland kirk; Berry Wall, the king of the Saratoga dudes, who had recently won a bet that he would appear in forty different costumes between breakfast and dinner on a single day; Mark Twain, who often visited the hotel to shoot billiards with his friend William Dean Howells, and whose white suits were consequently spotted with light blue billiard chalk; and August Belmont, short and stout, with a gleaming bald head and gray side whiskers, carrying himself imperiously as befitted a man who believed himself to be the monarch of all he surveyed. In addition I recognized two United States senators and three representatives, a major-general and two brigadiers, an admiral, a Supreme Court justice, a number of international courtesans, a Civil War hero and a world-famous inventor of farm machinery.

I did not see Mrs. Murchison or her companion.

A little after noon the papers arrived, and I joined the line that quickly formed at the stationery counter. Purchasing a *Spirit of the Times*, I found myself a rocker on the piazza and turned the pages with anticipation.

I didn't recognize my column when I found it. I had to read the headlines twice before it communicated its meaning to me. Then I read the lead paragraphs in sheer sickening incredulity:

SCANDAL THREATENS SARATOGA

NAKED BODY FOUND IN DUMBWAITER OF RESORT HOTEL

Underworld Figures, Bizarre Swindles Shadow Race of the Year, Reporter Discovers!

SARATOGA SPRINGS, N.Y.—The historic match race between The Mogul and Tenstrike may be staged against a darkening background of murder and fraud, authorities of the luxurious spa believe. The brutal murder of a man whose unclothed corpse was discovered in a dumbwaiter of the United States Hotel early Wednesday morning, coupled with the presence of notorious underworld figures and reports of extravagant confidence games involving top social leaders, all suggest a developing scandal of epic proportions . . .

I closed my eyes and pressed my hands to my temples. There seemed to be a roaring in my ears like Niagara Falls as heard from inside a barrel going over the edge. My heart pounded, my stomach sank and the blood in my veins turned to water. My first instinct was to curl up in a ball and hide in my rocker. My second, only slightly more practical, was to hurry to my room and lock the door. My third, which I followed, was to read the rest of the column and then decide what to do about it.

The balance of the story was anticlimactic. Apparently Hochmuth had no sensational material of his own, and he used up all of mine in the first two paragraphs. From there on, the story was simply a description of the racing scene as contained in my two telegrams. I finished it and then read the lead a second time. It was still just as disastrous.

He's crucified me. People will be waiting in line for a crack at me. I'll be barred from Saratoga for life. No newspaper in the country will hire me. I'll be lucky if some plug-ugly puts me out of my misery.

I shook my head to clear it of morbid hysteria. The first practical question was Chief Winklemann. He had let me know what to expect if I brought scandal to Saratoga—assuming I left his office physically unscathed, I would be barred from the track and all local hotels, and thus be unable to continue doing my job. Hochmuth would be justified in firing me, and the apparent irresponsibility of my story would serve to blackball me from future jobs in the sporting press.

Very well. The answer to the first practical question, then, was to stay away from Chief Winklemann until I was in a position to persuade him not to banish me from Saratoga. The way to persuade him was, of course, to offer him information that would help him solve crimes and prevent greater scandals.

Where could I find it?

The starting point was an ancient leather notebook underneath the dirty laundry in the bottom dresser drawer in my room. In it I kept my list of sources, the names and addresses of everyone who had ever supplied me with information on a story.

If I'm going to get it, I'd better get it fast, I thought. I tore out the newspaper story, folded it and stuffed it in my pocket. Then I entered the hotel and walked rapidly across the lobby to the ornate staircase at the rear, momentarily expecting a heavy hand to descend on my shoulder. It was all I could do to keep myself from taking the steps two at a time.

Fortunately I had my room key in my pocket. I unlocked the door and took one step into the room, and then stopped as if I had run into a wall.

Seated on the bed, with her hands folded primly in her lap and her wide eyes regarding me with a mixture of shyness and hope, was Mr. Murchison's companion.

For a moment neither of us spoke, and then we both spoke at once. "Mr. Moretti—" she began.

"Miss Linley?" I asked.

She dropped her eyes. "Linnett, Kate Linnett," she corrected. "Mr. Moretti, please forgive me for this intrusion, and please believe I don't make a practice of entering men's hotel rooms, unasked or otherwise. But"—she raised her eyes and fixed me with her level gaze—"I've come to apologize, and to ask for your help."

I saw that her eyes were not gray, as I had thought, but hazel, flecked with green. her heavy lustrous hair was exactly the color of a buckeye when you've polished it against

your nose, and her creamy skin was touched by a warm
pink blush. I waved her apology away.

"No apology necessary—but I would like to know how
you got into my room."

"The chambermaid was here. I persuaded her to let me
stay." She didn't say how. "Don't be angry. I had to see
you. I have a terrible problem, and I can't think of anyone
else who can help me."

"This wouldn't have anything to do with my article in
The Spirit of the Times, would it?"

The question surprised her. "Your article? No, I don't
know anything about your article. Why?"

"Nothing. You wouldn't have had time to read it any-
how." I sat down on the edge of the room's only chair.
"All right, Miss Linnett. I can give you about two minutes, and then I have to be gone from here. How can I
help you?"

"First, let me apologize. No, listen—in the lobby the
other day, when you asked me if we had ever met, I lied
to you. I knew very well who you were. I remembered you
as clearly as if—as if it hadn't been a week since the last
time I'd seen you."

"I knew it! I knew I couldn't have imagined it! It was—"
I paused, as I ransacked my memory for the specific time
and place. "It was—where was it?"

One side of her mouth turned up in gentle mockery.
"Don't you remember, Mr. Moretti?"

"Of course I do. It was—" *It had to be long ago,* I
thought. *Back before she looked the way she looks now. I
never would have forgotten her the way she looks now.* "It
was in Goshen! When we were kids in Goshen, Ohio!
Wasn't it?"

She nodded. "I don't blame you for forgetting. You were
three or four years older, which seemed like a generation
back then. And we had different friends, and my family

moved away after a year. I don't suppose you ever said more than two words to me, but—'' her voice lowered until it was almost inaudible—''for some reason I remember you very clearly.''

I drew a deep breath. ''Then why did you say you didn't know me?''

''By the time you asked me, I had found out that you were a newspaperman. And Mrs. Murchison, the lady who employs me—Mrs. Murchison doesn't want to have anything to do with newspapermen. She's had some unhappy experiences with newspaper publicity.''

''You mean because of the séances she runs for wealthy society ladies?''

She gasped and her eyes opened wide. ''How do you know about that?''

''Oh, I have my sources too, Kate.'' I spoke her first name tentatively and watched her face for a negative reaction, but there was none. ''The séances are something I want to talk to you about. But later. Right now I have to get out of here before the police arrive.'' I pulled open my bottom drawer and extracted the source notebook from under a dirty shirt, then drew Kate Linnett from the bed. ''What's your room number?''

''Three-twelve. Mrs. Murchison's next door, in three-ten.'' She looked at me in alarm. ''But why do you have to leave so quickly? I haven't told you about the money yet!''

I hesitated. ''What money?'' I asked.

''The bonds! The hundred and twenty thousand dollars' worth of bearer bonds!''

''The hundred and twenty-thousand—Oh, hell! I can't wait to hear about it now! Winklemann's probably on his way over here right this minute. If he catches me before I'm ready, I'll never get within a hundred miles of Saratoga again!'' I pulled her from the room after me and locked the door, slipping the key in my pocket. We walked down the corridor to the stairway. Kate was tall and straight beside me, her eyes only an inch or two below my own. "I'll come by your room as soon as I can, probably in about two hours. Will that be all right?" I asked.

"Yes, but knock quietly. Mrs. Murchison is ill, but she has ears like a cat." She glanced at me questioningly. "If the police are looking for you, won't they be watching the hotel?"

"Not the loading dock or the service stairs, I hope."

She turned off at the third-floor landing. Gambling that I still had a minute or two before Chief Winklemann could arrive from his office, I continued down the grand staircase into the lobby. I proceeded safely across it and out of the building, signaled the nearest cab waiting by the wide front steps and gave the driver an address. then I sank back in the seat, at least partially hidden from outside view.

Ten minutes later the cab delivered me to the home of Taffy the Welshman.

Taffy's real name was Hugh Llewellyn, but few people on either side of the law would have known it. Until his retirement two or three years before, he had been a top Pinkerton agent, a job which he held for the last decade of his working life. Before that, he had been for greater or lesser periods, coal miner, merchant seaman, job printer, small-town policeman, labor spy, Union soldier, smuggler, carnival barker and snake oil salesman, dynamiter and itinerant preacher. Since, during each period of his colorful past he had maintained relations (professional or otherwise) with the seamy side of society, and since he was gifted with an excellent memory, his knowledge of the underworld was encyclopedic.

I first met Taffy in Chicago while he was breaking up a crooked gambling ring at one of the tracks. I gave him and his employer some excellent publicity, and he was grateful enough to share his knowledge with me on two or three subsequent occasions.

He loved horse racing and he loved gambling, so it was not surprising that he had chosen Saratoga Springs for his retirement home. He lived alone in a small bungalow set back from the street under two great elm trees. He met me on the flagstone path before I could reach the front door.

"Well, Paddy, this is an unexpected pleasure," he cried in the high tenor voice, which emerged so incongruously from his big square body. "Who do you like in the match race?"

I told him The Mogul, except for the odds. He agreed the odds were rotten, and said he was tempted to skip the race entirely. I said that might be the wise thing to do. He showed me into his home, which was neatly and sparsely appointed, and asked me what I would drink. When I was leaning back in a Morris chair with a tall Irish whiskey in my hand, he rubbed his hands together, scowled, and said, "Enough of this small talk and la-di-da. What do you want to ask me about?"

I told him briefly about my problems with Hochmuth, Isaac Murphy's uneasiness concerning the upcoming race, the body in the dumbwaiter and Chief Winklemann's aversion to publicity. "Now, for reasons I don't need to bore you with, today's issue of *The Spirit of the Times* contains an article that begins as follows." I pulled the clipping from my pocket and read the headlines and opening paragraph aloud. Taffy regarded me impassively from pale blue eyes fringed with colorless lashes. When I finished, he shook his head regretfully.

"You were drunk. You took refuge from your problems in liquor. I have no doubt you sent off a pack of lies and half-truths to your editor to buy time for yourself, didn't you? And look where it's gotten you. Winklemann will skin you with a dull knife. Decent men will turn away when you enter a room, and women will shudder and hide their eyes. It's a lesson for us all. I'm only sorry it has to be you who provides it."

I swallowed some of my Irish, which seemed to taste a good deal like kerosene. "Everything you say is absolutely true. Wine is a mocker and strong drink is raging. I've learned my lesson, and I'll never, never do it again." I paused and lowered my eyes, suggesting penitence. "Now, what I was wondering was—" I resumed.

"What you were wondering was," he interrupted, "could I help you find something to trade to Winklemann so he'll go easy on you."

"That's true. What a knack you have for getting right down to the heart of the matter."

I had only used a touch of the brogue, but it was enough to make him wince. "If you talk like that anymore, I won't give you the time of day. Now first tell me about the body. Describe it as completely as you can."

He listened intently as I told him everything I could remember about the corpse under the starched sheet. His wide, ruddy face was set in an expression of concentration, and the pale eyes seemed to bore into my own. When I finished, he grunted.

"You say he was shaved between the eyebrows. What about the skin on his face? Was it rough, coarse? What about his pores? Were they bigger than you'd expect?"

I thought. "The skin was rough, yes. And the pores might have been a little bigger than average. Why, what does that mean?"

He ignored my question. "I don't suppose he had a gold earring in his right ear, did he?"

"Of course not! If he had, don't you think I would have mentioned it?" Then I remembered something, and continued in a milder tone. "Come to think of it, though, there was a spot in the middle of his right earlobe. I thought it was a freckle, but it could have been a small hole, I guess.''

Taffy betrayed his satisfaction with the slightest of smiles. ''It was, Paddy, it was. He started wearing that earring when he was twelve years old. All the boys in his gang in New Orleans wore them, and woe betide anyone who made fun of them about it.''

''Who is he, Taffy?''

''Unless I'm very much mistaken, his name is, or was, Frog Robinette. When he graduated from the Pontchartrain Tigers he joined a carnival as a roustabout, and then found he had some talent as a performer. He toured with various traveling shows for four or five years, sharpening his skills and enjoying the applause. I ran into him once in St. Paul, Minnesota. He was doing the Half Man—Half Woman— you know, a few peeks on the outside, and inside he shows you both sets of plumbing—and doing it pretty well. That night I caught him cheating at cards. It was a family game, so he had to leave the show.

''I'd hear of him every so often after that. He went into the con. For a while he was working with the Foul-Mouthed Kid in Davenport, Iowa—they were roping marks for a fight store there. Once I heard he was playing the badger game with Foureyes Mooney in Louisville, and another time somebody saw him with Duke Ramirez in San Antonio . . .''

''Taffy,'' I interrupted, ''how do you know it's Frog Robinette on the slab down there?''

''Oh, I don't *know* it, but I'd be willing to take bets,'' he said complacently. ''The eyebrows, the coloring, the big white teeth, the earring hole, the skin and pores—''

''But what about the skin and pores?''

''Theatrical make-up, Paddy! Don't you know they use white lead in it? A few years of plastering that stuff on your face every night and your skin looks like the surface of the moon. Then you have to keep using more make-up to cover up the damage. You can always tell somebody who's been a professional actor if you can get close to him when he's got his make-up off.''

''Was he on the legitimate stage long enough to ruin his skin?'' It seemed to me Robinette was too young for all the experiences Taffy was crediting him with.

''He didn't have to be. He used make-up in the con. He'd make an appearance as a white-haired old cattle baron, or a dying millionaire or a rich recluse with a grudge against the government—anything, he didn't care. The trickier the better. Why, in the badger game he even played the girl, and when he and Ramirez were working the Prisoner in San Antonio—''

I spilled most of my drink on my lap. ''Working the Prisoner? What do you mean, working the Prisoner?''

Taffy looked at me in surprise. ''Why, the Spanish Prisoner. Haven't you ever heard of the Spanish Prisoner?'' My blank expression was answer enough. ''Paddy, I'm surprised at you! Of all the con games currently in use— barring salted gold mines and the old money-box dodge— the Spanish Prisoner has the longest whiskers. Really, you mean to tell me you've never heard of it?''

''Not until I got here day before yesterday.''

His eyes narrowed. ''Has it got something to do with this Robinette thing?''

''Your guess is as good as mine. Probably a damn sight better, as a matter of fact. Tell me about it.''

He described the operation of this venerable swindle, of which for some reason I had never heard; the victim, or mark, is ''roped'' by one of the confidence men, who secures his friendship and trust in any one of a number of time-proven ways. When the roper feels the mark is ready, he arranges for an accidental meeting with his partner, the inside man. The inside man is playing the role of a Spanish grandee, exiled from his native land by a tyrannical government. (He may just as well be Mexican, Moroccan, Turkish or Croatian, as long as the nationality he claims makes his story—and accent—believable.) The grandee unfolds his unhappy tale to the mark and roper. He tells them that the immensely rich nobleman who was his patron in the old country is now imprisoned, held incommunicado by the tyrant, who hopes to force him to relinquish his great wealth. The nobleman's spirit is unbroken, however, and he has persuaded one of his jailers to open a line of communications with his faithful servitor, the grandee.

The nobleman has sent a message that his escape can be arranged for a certain sum of money. If he were free, he could easily raise that sum ten times over from his own funds—but while he is in prison, there is no way for him to touch his wealth. The grandee is desperately borrowing money and selling the family jewels to raise money for his patron, but he doubts he will be able to raise enough.

Impatiently, I hurried the description along. "So the roper persuades the mark to put up the money, with the understanding he'll be paid a big bonus when the nobleman's out of prison—"

"Not quite. The roper also agrees to put up some money. Why not? What has he got to lose?"

"All right, they both put up money. Then the next morning, poof! The roper and the grandee are both gone, and the mark is staring into an empty pocketbook."

"No again. They've got the fish on the hook now, and they want to play him. Besides, if they kissed him off like that, he'd probably go to the police, and they want to avoid that if they can. So they keep the story going. The money is raised, and the grandee takes it to deliver to his agent. Then nightly, for three or four nights, reports from the agent arrive in code. The mark and the roper are present as each message is decoded. The plan appears to be moving as planned; the necessary payments have been made to

A and B, transportation has been arranged and so forth. Then, at the eleventh hour, betrayal! The plan is discovered, the corrupt jailer is arrested and the nobleman is transferred to another prison. And the money is, of course, irrevocably gone.'' Taffy smiled like an art connoisseur regarding a particularly fine etching.

''And the mark never gets wise to the swindle?''

''If the con men know their stuff, the mark is convinced that the mix-up was an act-of-God accident which could never happen again. So they send him back home to raise another stake. Then, two or three months later, back he comes with another ten or twenty thousand dollars in his poke, all ready to do it again.''

I digested this while Taffy shuffled to the sideboard to replenish my Irish. he wasn't drinking himself; one of the few consequences of his unwholesome life was a heart condition that couldn't tolerate alcohol. He regarded me closely as he handed me the glass. ''All right, now what's the Spanish Prisoner got to do with Robinette's death?''

I told him about Sharples' cryptic allusions to ''prisoners'' at Dirty Helen's. ''It may not mean anything, but it's an interesting coincidence,'' I said. He nodded his head in agreement and sank back into his chair with a sigh. I remembered a fact that I always tended to forget when I was around him: he was an old man.

I told him I had seen Gus Gibbons at the track. He agreed that Gibbons was quite capable of being involved in any shenanigans currently developing in Saratoga, but could think of nothing specific against the man—''barring his morals, his personal habits, his character and his appearance,'' he added.

We talked a few more minutes, and then I rose to go. An expression of disappointment crossed his face. ''So soon? I thought you might take another glass with me, Paddy.''

''I'm afraid I better keep moving, Taffy. There are still

some questions I want to ask before I have to talk to Chief Winklemann. Which reminds me—what's your personal opinion of him?''

"A good tough policeman, as far as I know. They say he's kept Saratoga reasonably honest, which is no mean accomplishment in a gambling town.'' He rose and walked to the door with me. For the first time I noticed that the seat of his trousers was shiny and a tear in his shirt had been amateurishly mended. Taffy the Welshman's retirement was something less than luxurious, I thought.

"Don't wait till you need help on a story,'' he said he we shook hands. "Come see me anytime—I'm almost always home.''

I tired not to notice the entreaty on his big, tired face. "I will, Taffy, I will,'' I said, wondering if I ever would unless I needed to know something more.

Walking down the quiet residential street toward the bustling activity of Broadway, I outlined my situation to myself. Assuming Taffy was right, I knew the identity of the body in the dumbwaiter—Frog Robinette. But there was the possibility that Taffy was wrong. There was also the possibility that Chief Winklemann had already discovered the body's identity from other sources. In either case telling him Robinette's name would do me no good whatever. *No, I need more,* I thought, *I need to talk to Sharples. And if there really is something funny about the match race, I need to talk to Ike Murphy, and to Harrison Fowler and the Dunne Brothers, if possible.*

And, of course, to Kate Linnett, I added with a tingle of excitement. *A hundred and twenty thousand dollars is a lot of money!*

At the corner I raised my hand to signal an empty cab, and gave the driver his directions.

4

Problems and Consolations
of a Fugitive

Sometimes trying to find people is the surest way of missing them. Afterward you realize that just sitting down in the street and waiting for them to stumble over you would have produced better results. But, alas, that's afterward.

Sharples was nowhere around the track, not in the stands, in the clubhouse, in the paddock or the betting ring—at least not when I was there. In the process of searching for him, with my handkerchief held up to mask the lower part of my face in hopes that I would be taken for a man with a bad cold, the August heat notwithstanding, I had two close brushes with Captain Winklemann's police. The first time, I noticed an officer moving toward me with a purposeful expression on his shining red face. We were in the grandstand, standing in the aisle, and he was twenty feet above me. Moving quickly through the crowd toward the exit corridor, I was able to reach open space ten seconds before he did, and I was out the gate and out of sight before he was free of the throng.

The second time was a closer squeak. It happened about

forty-five minutes later, near the fence beside the betting ring. Searching the crowd around the bookmakers with my eyes, I had absent-mindedly lowered my handkerchief. I felt a heavy tap on the shoulder, and a gruff but polite voice said in my ear, "Excuse, sir, but would you mind telling me your name?"

"Why certainly, officer," I said to the mustachioed policeman behind me. "Samuel J. Silliphant, with two l's. I have a livery business in Springfield, Missouri, a twelve-room house and a wife and four children. I belong to the Mount Olivet Baptist Church and always vote the straight Republican ticket. What else would you like to know?"

He studied me suspiciously as I rattled off this nonsense, tugging at one side of his guardsman's mustache and peering through tiny bloodshot eyes. "Have you got anything that proves who you are?" he asked when I finished.

"Why, certainly. Just a second." I turned partly away from him and put one hand into my breast pocket. "I think you'll find this satisfactory—" Then I was off, running and dodging through the crowd as if I were back in the relay races at the Corbo County Fair. The policeman was after me almost instantly. He was a big, heavy man, and slow of foot but quicker-witted than his brother officer had been. It didn't take him long to remember his whistle, and in a few moments its damned piercing skirl was calling attention to my flight and summoning assistance in my capture.

From ahead I heard an answering whistle. The path in front of me opened as spectators drew away on both sides. At the far end of the path, near the grandstand, another policeman came running toward me, whistling furiously. I veered to the right, and for a moment was concealed in the crowd again.

Then suddenly a familiar face materialized before me, and simultaneously a thrust-out foot snaked in between my own. *May God roast your liver in Hell, Gus Gibbons!* I cried to myself as I cartwheeled through the air and landed on the back of my neck on the grass.

Gibbons pounced upon me like a fat cat on a dazed bird. "I've got him! I've got him!" he shouted. He put one knee on my chest and tried to secure my hands. Grinning, a thread of saliva dangling from his lips, he grunted malignantly, "What are you running away from, Moretti?"

My right hand was still free, and I used it to answer. I hit him behind the ear, a beautifully clean, resonant clout. His eyes bugged out like a gigged frog's. He opened his mouth, but no sound emerged. Slowly he inclined to the side, and his fat knee slid off my chest.

I writhed out from under him and began running again. Now I could hear a third whistle twittering from somewhere on my right. The crowd thinned out as I moved around the rear of the grandstand, and suddenly I was pounding along the back of the building alone.

"Paddy—in here!" cried a voice from a doorway down a short flight of steps. Instinctively I leaped toward it, reaching its shelter before the pursuing police rounded the corner. The heavy door slammed behind me.

Gasping for breath, I peered at my rescuer in the dim light. It was Isaac Murphy. He was dressed in racing silks, pink and dark green, and held a large Havana cigar in one hand.

"Ike—police—right behind me—" I gasped.

"I know. Come on, now!" He seized my arm and drew me along a short hall to another door, which was passed through and closed behind us. We ran down another short corridor and around a corner. A dark, narrow stairway led downward.

"They'll never find you down here," the little jockey said as he preceded me down the steep stairs. "We're down underneath the stands. Most people don't even know there's rooms down here." In the crepuscular light I could barely see that I was in a large area apparently used for storage. There was a pile of lumber near one wall.

Murphy established me behind the lumber. "I've got a race in about three minutes, Paddy, so you just stay here till I get back. You'll be safe here till then. Afterward, we can figure what to do about you."

"Ike, I promise you, I'm not guilty of anything."

His white teeth flashed against his coppery skin, now chocolate brown in the half-light. "Why, Lord Almighty, I know that!"

After he left, I sat with my back against the stacked boards and listened for the sound of approaching policemen. I thought I could hear running feet somewhere above me, and shouting voices. Then after a few minutes I could not hear them anymore. The only noise beside my own breathing was the great susurration of the crowd in the grandstands above, rising and falling like the distant roar of an ocean.

My thoughts turned again to Otto Hochmuth. *A beast of a man he is, to crucify a fellow who is the sole support of a widowed mother and four helpless young sisters,* complained the Irish poet in me. *But you don't have a widowed mother and four sisters,* the inner Yankee reporter pointed out. *Ahhh—but did he know that?* the Irish poet cried.

When Isaac Murphy returned I didn't hear him until his hand touched my arm. It is not easy to leap six inches in the air from a sitting position, but I accomplished it. "Do you want to give a man heart failure?" I asked when I returned to earth.

"Sorry," he said with a grin. He squatted down beside me comfortably. "Now tell me what you've gotten yourself into." He had changed out of his riding silks and was wearing an elegantly cut suit of some very light color and a flowered satin vest. His shoes were Congress gaiters, lustrously polished. A large diamond on his ring finger reflected all the available light. Somehow he seemed as much at home here, surrounded by piled lumber, as he would have been in the bar of the Newport Jockey Club.

"Did you win the race?" I asked.

"Oh, yes. Won by two lengths. One more than I told the owner I'd win by. Now tell me why you got policemen blowing whistles after you."

I told him about the story in *The Spirit of the Times,* and what Chief Winklemann had threatened to do to me if I brought scandal to Saratoga Springs. When I finished, he shook his head.

"Seems to me you're just making it worse for yourself by running away. He's going to get you sooner or later. What's the point of riling him up worse than he was?"

I explained that if I could find out some facts Winklemann didn't know, he might be willing to withdraw his decree of banishment. "I've already got one piece of information that may help. I think I know the name of the man who was killed at the United States Hotel: Frog Robinette."

"Don't mean a thing to me," Murphy said.

"It may to Winklemann, though. This Robinette was a confidence man, and probably has a record a mile long. Now if I could just find out what he was doing here in Saratoga—"

"Most people come to Saratoga in August to bet on the horses, or to get money from other people who bet on the horses. Either way, there's horses in it," Murphy mused.

"And the biggest race of the meet is your Mogul-Tenstrike match this Saturday. What about it, Ike—do you still feel that pressure you were talking about?

He nodded. His expression was grave, sphinxlike. "Yeah, I feel it stronger than ever, but I can't put a name to it. I don't like it. It's—it's—I'll tell you one thing, Paddy—after this, I'm never going to ride for Mr. Fowler again!''

''Why not?''

''There's some people that try to make everybody else feel small. It's like they just can't bear for a man to stand up straight around them—they got to have everybody feeling guilty about something. Guilty about being poor, or dumb, or ugly—guilty about being black—'' He stopped, and when he spoke again, his voice was coolly matter-of-fact. ''He's not a gentleman I care for personally.''

''I believe it.'' A thought occurred to me. ''Say, how did you happen to be there by the door when I came by? You must have the best Ouija board in the country!''

''Sometimes I take a cigar and step out behind the grandstand before a race. It's quieter there than in the jockey room. When I saw you come around that corner with them whistles blowing behind you, I realized the Lord was moving in mysterious ways again.''

''Amen. Now the next question: How am I going to get out of here?''

Murphy smiled, as at some secret joke. ''Why, you're not, not for a while. You're going to stay down here till after the last race, when the biggest crowds are going out the gates. Then you and me are going to walk right out as bold as brass, right in front of those policemen, and get ourselves a carriage and ride into town.'' He rose to his feet. ''Now you stay put, and I'll be back in ten minutes.''

''Are you crazy?'' I cried. He waved his hand and disappeared behind the piled lumber.

Ten minutes later he was back, as promised. He was carrying an old alpaca jacket, a candle, a packet of lucifers and three winebottle corks. He lit the candle and set it on the floor, then took off his coat and rolled up his shirt sleeves. ''Sit back and relax, Paddy, and before you know

it, you will have joined the colored race," he said as he
turned one of the corks in the candle's flame.

He applied the char smoothly to my face, working it in
above my hairline and right up to my eyelashes. He went
into my ears as far as he could go, and down my neck well
below my collar. "Yes, sir—when I get done with you,
your own mamma wouldn't recognize you."

"Ike, what's it like to be colored?" I asked. "If I really
were, what would I be thinking when I walked out the
gates?"

"Oh, the same kind of things white folks think—you're
tired, you're hungry, you sure will be glad to get home to
your woman and your children." He was silent a moment,
his strong fingers working the blackness into my skin. "No,
that's not exactly right," he said thoughtfully. "The colored man's been working all day, and the white man's been
playing. So the white man, he's thinking about the money
he won and how he's going to spend it, or the money he
lost and how he's going to win it back tomorrow. But the
black man, he's counting the days till Sunday. And also
he's being very careful not to accidentally bump into any
white folks."

"How much bad feeling is there toward whites?"

"Not so much. A couple of years ago I would have said
hardly any. Mostly it's the other way around—the white
have the bad feelings. I can't understand it. Why, when I
was a boy back on Mr. Williams' farm in Lexington, whites
and coloreds would drink out of the same dipper and never
think anything about it. Today in some railroad stations
they have different drinking faucets. Some places down
South they make the coloreds sit in the back of the horse-
cars, sit up in the top balcony of theaters, use different
toilets and sit on different park benches. There never was
anything like that ten years ago. But lately it seems like
some politicians are trying to make white people believe

they always hated colored people." He shook his head in puzzlement. "And a lot of white people *are* believing it. Like they don't have any memory of how things really were."

He finished my head and neck and asked me to roll up my sleeves. As he rubbed char on my wrists I asked, "There isn't that kind of feeling up here in the North, is there?"

"Nowhere near as much, and not hardly any against me, or the other black jockeys. Oh, every once in a while you see somebody like Jackie McCandless looking for ways to bad-mouth us. Or Mister Fowler—but mostly they couldn't treat us nicer if we was white. But you don't see many of us riding on tracks down South."

He stepped back to admire his craftsmanship as I rolled my sleeve down over my darkened wrists, and buttoned the cuffs with blackened fingers. "I declare, I believe you'll pass, Paddy!" he said with a wide grin.

I slipped on the alpaca jacket while he turned my suit coat inside out and folded it over his arm. Then he blew out the candle, and we left the sanctuary.

As we emerged into daylight Murphy inspected me closely. "It's good your hair's kind of kinky. Nothing we can do about your blue eyes except let your eyelids droop down like you're sleepy and keep your head bent. When you walk don't raise your feet more than an inch off the ground. And slouch your shoulders."

We walked toward the carriage turn-around. Murphy strode with a buoyant step, smiling and returning salutations, and I shuffled beside him, concentrating on appearing as unremarkable as possible. Under lowered eyelids I studied the faces that appeared before me; their eyes slid over me like water over a smooth rock.

Murphy signaled to a cab driver. As he started to step

up into the cab, another man, pushing forward to occupy
the same vehicle, collided with him on the step.

"Where do you think you're going?" the man asked
rudely. "I signaled this cab first! Just because you're a
jockey, you think you can lord it over white men?"

My heart stood still. It was Gus Gibbons, with a lump
the size of an orange swelling lividly behind his ear.

With a courteous bow Isaac Murphy stepped down from
the step and gestured to Gibbons to enter. "My error, sir.
I'll take another carriage," he said.

Gibbons glared at him, then at me, then back to him.
"Damned uppity coons—just remember this is a white
man's world," he said over his shoulder as he seated himself in the cab.

"Gentlemen like you keep me from forgetting," Murphy said in a voice too low to carry. "Shall we take the
next hack in line, friend Rastus?"

We took our place in the procession of carriages returning to Saratoga Springs. Murphy was bound for his boardinghouse on the far side of the town, and I asked him to
drop me off by the rear of the United States Hotel. We
stopped at one end of the loading dock, which I was glad
to see was empty.

"Do you know what you're going to do?" the jockey
asked.

"I plan to pay a call on a young lady." I shook his hand.
"A million thanks, Ike. The disguise is perfect. I had no
idea a dark skin could do so much to hide a man."

"It's a fact my people have known for some time,"
Murphy said dryly. "Good luck, Paddy. Don't forget to
shuffle."

I entered the hotel through a door on the loading dock.
Inside were the hotel's great storage rooms, where meats
and vegetables. wines and liquors, linens and rugs, statues,
paintings and furniture were stored until needed. In one

room the size of a tennis court, beeves hung from hooks as close together as worshipers in a church. In another, cases of whiskey, gin, rum and brandy were stacked higher than my head. It made me feel like a virtuous glutton who has died and gone to heaven.

Since it was almost the dinner hour I avoided the store-rooms that connected with the kitchens. By a combination of stealth and luck I at last arrived at a service stairway. I hesitated a moment, listening for the sound of footsteps on the stairs above me, but there were none. Carefully I began my ascent to the third floor.

I met no one on the stairs. At the third floor I passed into the residential part of the hotel, and immediately found myself in a busy, bustling corridor, full of dignified gentle-men and their ladies of fashion and their petulant children, returning from an afternoon outing or setting out for the evening meal. I concentrated on shuffling again, reading the numbers on doors from the corner of my eye—352—336—328—the corridor turned and became more crowded as it neared the grand staircase—320—316—finally, 312. I tapped lightly on the panel.

"Yes? Who is it?" Instead of answering I tapped again. After a few seconds the door opened and Kate Linnett stared out at me. Her face registered surprise, then disap-pointment. "Oh—what is it? What do you want?"

"Got a message for you from Mr. Moretti, ma'am," I said in a minstrel show accent. "He said I was to give it to you personal."

Her eyes widened in recognition, and she stepped back from the door. "Why, then come in," she said huskily. I shuffled past her, my shoes making a scuffling sound on the rug. The bustle in the hall was abruptly cut off as she closed the door.

"What in the world are you doing in blackface?" she asked.

I considered answering with a brief buck-and-wing and abandoned the idea. "I'm trying to keep clear of the Chief of Police. So far, it seems to be working."

"I didn't think you were coming. I've been waiting for you all afternoon." She glanced toward the connecting door between her room and the next. "And please speak softly—she's asleep now, but she could wake up at any time."

She was wearing a white piqué robe and blue satin slippers. Her auburn hair was loose around her shoulders. As if aware of my admiring gaze, she pulled the robe tighter around her body—a misguided kind of modesty, I thought, since it modeled her fine breasts and slender waist in high relief. She gestured to me to sit down.

"How did you know about our séances?" she asked abruptly.

"What did you mean about a hundred and twenty thousand dollars' worth of bearer bonds?" I countered.

She studied my face for a moment. "I'm going to have to trust you, Paddy. I don't have anyone else to go to. A terrible thing has happened to Mrs. Murchison and to me. She's so upset about it she hasn't gotten out of bed for two days. If we can't make everything right again, I'm afraid she'll stay in bed the rest of her life."

"Why don't you tell me about it from the beginning?"

She regarded me levelly and nodded her head. "Yes, I will. When Mrs. Murchison's husband died six years ago, the largest single part of his estate was a portfolio of bonds. At the time they had a face value of a hundred and fifty thousand dollars; since then some of them have matured and been cashed in. As of the day before yesterday there was a hundred twenty thousand dollars' worth left in the portfolio, which was, as a matter of fact, a green oilskin envelope Mrs. Murchison kept underneath her writing paper in a desk drawer."

"She kept a hundred and twenty thousand dollars' worth of bonds in a hotel room desk drawer?"

"Mrs. Murchison doesn't believe in banks. Or hotel safes." She took three or four steps toward the door, then retraced them back toward the bed. She rubbed her hands together in agitation. "Paddy, the income from those bonds is almost everything Mrs. Murchison has in the world, and whoever has them can get every cent of it just by clipping off the coupons—"

"Or selling the bonds at any brokerage office," I interrupted.

"—or selling them at any brokerage office. They're absolutely negotiable. That's why we've got to find them, and find them fast, while they're still here in Saratoga."

"You mean, *if* they're still here in Saratoga. By this time they could just as easily be in New York or Chicago." I shook my head. "And if they are still in town—"

She stopped me with a gesture of her hand. "Shhh— Mrs. Murchison's awake." She walked quickly to the connecting door and opened it. "I'm here, Mrs. M.," she said in a soothing voice. "What can I get you?" The door closed behind her.

The income on $120,000, I reflected, was somewhere between $6000 and $8000 a year. A more than comfortable amount of money for an elderly lady living in her own home, but hardly enough to keep two people summering at places like the United States Hotel for very long. The séance business must make up a substantial part of their income.

From the next room I could hear Kate's voice, low-pitched and reassuring, and another, querulously interrupting her. It was impossible to make out individual words, but from the tone of both voices Kate was succeeding in calming the old lady down.

After five minutes she returned, closing the door quietly

behind her. She held one finger to her lips. "Be very quiet," she whispered. "I gave her medicine and a sleeping powder. She'll be asleep soon."

She sat down on the edge of her bed, and we looked at each other. Her lovely face had a tense and hunted look. She rubbed one hand across her forehead, sighed and folded her hands in her lap. Slowly the tenseness left her face, and the beginning of a smile touched her lips. "Do you want a cloth to wipe off that burnt cork with? The cards said I was going to meet a tall dark man, but I don't think they meant *that* dark."

I had forgotten what an incongruous spectacle I must be. "Oh, yes, of course. I'm sorry." I started to rise, but she stood up first and went to the washstand in the corner, where she poured water into the porcelain bowl and dampened a washcloth in it.

"Here, let me," she said, rubbing the cloth over my face and neck. "Raise your head so I can get under your chin. Close your eyes, now—" The cloth moved briskly over my skin, pausing to be wrung out and then resuming its progress. She worked as competently as a hospital nurse. The smell of her reminded me of a shady garden in the early summer. When she finished with my head she stepped back to inspect her handiwork. "There. I believe that's a face I recognize." She handed me the washcloth. "You can finish your hands and wrists yourself."

I washed and dried my hands, and felt ready to take advantage of any opportunity that might present itself. I sat on the edge of the bed a foot away from her. "There's something I don't understand," I began. "Why do you need me? Why don't you and Mrs. Murchison go to the police? After all, theft is against the law, and that's what they're for."

"I knew you'd ask that. It isn't easy to tell you." She paused, and I moved reassuringly toward her. She appeared not to notice. "It's the séances you asked about, Paddy. I don't know how you heard about them, but it's true, Mrs. Murchison does possess unusual gifts, and she often puts them at the disposal of friends. She's not a professional, you understand. She doesn't do it for the money. It's just that many of them are wealthy, and they know she's not, and they—give her things."

"Things like money?" I moved again, so that our thighs were touching.

"Money sometimes. Sometimes jewelry, knickknacks, trinkets. Never anything very valuable." She stood up and walked across the room and back. "But the police in Newport heard about it when we were there last year and didn't understand at all. They acted like Mrs. Murchison was some kind of swindler. You have no idea how insulting they were! They said we were lucky not to go to jail, that we were to leave Newport and not come back. It was so humiliating for Mrs. M. She swore she'd never have anything to do with the police again."

"I can understand that," I said gently, "especially if she has reason to think the Newport police had her blacklisted in the other resorts, like Saratoga Springs, for example." I paused; when she didn't say anything, I prodded: "Is that what happened, Kate?"

"I'm afraid so. They said that's what they were going to do. They said they were sending our names to the other resort police departments, and if we ever got into trouble they'd know about it and put us in jail." She had stopped pacing and now stood in the center of the room. "So you see, we can't go to the police. They wouldn't help us— they'd probably accuse us of stealing the money in the first place."

I reached out my hand and took hers. It lay motionless in mine. I drew her gently toward the bed, and she sat down beside me. I continued holding her hand. "I'll do anything I can for you, but I don't know how I can help. I'm not a detective, Kate, and I can't afford to have anything more to do with the police than you can. It's all I can do just to stay out from under Chief Winklemann."

She turned to me and her fingers squeezed mine. "Paddy, the biggest thing in Saratoga is gambling—gambling on horses and gambling in casinos. Isn't it likely that whoever stole our bonds will use them for gambling?" Her eyes were wide, the irises like hazel and green agates. "You can find out who is betting more than he ought to be, or paying off debts he shouldn't be able to. You've got all kinds of people who tell you things—all newspaper reporters do. And when we find out who took the bonds—" she hesitated indecisively, then rushed on—"we'll get them back somehow."

I was intensely aware of her proximity. Her parted lips were only inches from my own. "Get them back how?" I asked huskily. "What do you mean, somehow?" Instead of answering, she closed her eyes. The pressure of her fingers tightened, and my mouth moved toward hers like filings to a magnet. Her lips were soft, warm, gently suggestive. Then, as my arms slipped around her and her hands clasped behind my neck, they were suddenly hot and demanding. Her firm breasts pressed against my chest, and she pivoted on her hip to bring her belly and thighs tight against mine. Together we sank back on the bed. "Oh, Paddy—" she whispered as I tore my mouth from hers and buried my face in the cool, smooth flesh between her breasts. "Oh, Paddy, we mustn't—"

"Sssh." I raised my mouth to hers again as I fumbled with the belt on her robe. I found both ends and gave an exultant tug to release the bowknot, just as she broke off the kiss and struggled up on one elbow.

"Wait—listen!" she commanded. The blood was pounding so hard in my ears I couldn't have heard the walls falling, but I obediently froze. "It's Mrs. Murchison! She's awake again!" Regaining a sitting position, she called out, "I hear you, Mrs. M. I'll be in in a second."

We both stood up, and she reknotted her belt. "You have to go, Paddy. She won't go back to sleep now." She put her hands on my chest and looked at me with an expression that combined desire, sorrow and a kind of bittersweet humor. "I'm sorry, dear," she whispered. "But there'll be other days." Gently she pushed me toward the door. "Find out about the money." She kissed me quickly, and a moment later I was standing in the corridor. I heard her voice call, "I'm coming," and then the sound of the connecting door closing.

I looked around me. The wide hall, with its deep-pile carpeting and gilt-framed mirrors, was empty. Twenty or thirty feet to my left was the main staircase; up the great stairwell came the rumble of hundreds of voices from the lobby and the dining room beyond. I turned to the right and walked quickly back toward the service stairs. I reached them without meeting anyone.

At the head of the service stairway I paused and listened. All I could hear were the businesslike sounds of rattling crockery, banging pots and splashing water, and the imperious commands of chefs and their lieutenants. As I stood there on the landing, the smell, taste and feel of Kate Linnett swept my senses with such realism that my muscles twitched and my hair stood on end. I missed the uncompleted part of our lovemaking like a wounded soldier missing an amputated leg. *Ah, it may be the love of my life I'm leaving, and her as interested as I was in what was coming next.* I wondered how long it would be before I could see her alone again.

I walked rapidly and silently down the steps, meeting no one. At the first floor level I began retracing my steps of two hours earlier, working my way toward the loading platform by way of unoccupied storage rooms. I passed through three rooms without incident, feeling my way through semidarkness.

The fourth room was totally dark. It was, I remembered, the storage room in which beef carcasses hung from hooks in close, orderly rows. The air was cool and still. I moved into the room and followed the wall clockwise, the fingers of my left hand extended to touch the exit door when I reached it.

I was halfway around when I heard a noise behind me. It was a scraping sound, as if a piece of metal had struck masonry. A moment later a scuffling sound came from ahead of me and to my right.

I moved to the wall and stood with my back against it as I realized that at least two other persons shared the darkness with me.

5

Uncomfortable Encounters, Both Private and Public

Holding my breath and moving on tiptoe, I left the wall and stepped silently into the middle of the room. After three steps my outthrust hands encountered a beef carcass, smooth, damp and surprisingly cool. The thought of Frog Robinette flashed into my mind; no doubt he would feel much the same to the touch. My hands moved around the carcass to another less then a foot from the first, and then around it to a third. The darkness was impenetrable, and there was a faint sickish-sweet smell of blood in the still air.

Behind me I heard the scrape of leather on stone. As if in answer there was the sound of a stomach growling on my left. Yes, there were at least two men in the storage room with me, and not for the moment did I consider the possibility that their business here was innocent.

I took another step and moved past another hanging carcass. *Where are the knives and cleavers and meat-axes?* I asked myself. *They must be here—you can't butcher beef without them.* If I could get my hands on something with a cutting edge it would help to even the odds. Failing that, what else? I could yell for help, but I doubted if my voice would carry beyond the closed doors of the storage room, and even if it did, who knows how many empty rooms in this catacomb it would have to penetrate before it reached a pair of helpful ears? And of course the sound of my voice would pinpoint to Scrapefoot and Gutrumble . . .

Could I hide myself between two sides of beef? I could try—but I realized that would only postpone the moment of my discovery. Could I work my way back to one of the doors? Aside from the fact I was no longer sure where the doors were, that would require me to turn my back toward my pursuers, an unappealing prospect. So I was left with only one option: continuing on across the room carcass by carcass, until I found either a weapon or a way out.

My hands moved blindly around one clammy haunch, then another, then a third. Or maybe the clamminess came from the combination of cool beef and my own sweating palms. In any case, the third beef swung away, causing the chain that suspended it to creak with a grating squeal, like a drawbridge being raised over a moat. I froze at the sound. Behind me Scrapefoot broke his silence. "That's him!" he cried in a hoarse, triumphant voice. "Get him!"

The two pursuers thudded blindly toward me through the meat. It took a second for me to break my paralysis, then I began to run forward with my head lowered and my arms raised for protection. My progress was a series of stumbling lurches as I ricocheted from one carcass to another. My groping hands set the beeves to swinging and the chains to shrieking, and I could hear the men behind me curse as they thudded into the moving sides.

I don't know how long I groped my way through that damned bovine mausoleum before I reached the far wall— it felt like hours—but finally my fingers touched masonry. Quickly I began to work my way along the wall. My heart leaped as I realized the sounds of pursuit were moving to the left; now I was traveling at right angles to them and they didn't know it.

I had moved along the wall perhaps ten feet when something struck me in the solar plexus and knocked the breath out of me. I gave an audible gasp and lowered my hands. They encountered the smooth slate surface of a cutting bench.

My hands scrambled across the bench top searching for a weapon. Scrapefoot's voice called from the left, "Did you hear that? Get the bastard!" Footsteps approached. I groaned in frustration—the bench top seemed empty.

I drew a deep breath and suddenly was aware of a heavily sweet odor—a cloying smell that suggested hotel barrooms and barbershops. Then my right hand closed on the handle of something, and simultaneously Scrapefoot's hand closed on my left arm.

What I had found was not the knife or cleaver I was praying for—thank God—but a heavy wooden mallet or maul. I whipped it through a short arc and it struck my attacker somewhere in the side of back. He grunted, swore, released my arm and found my neck with his hands.

I heard another voice call, "Face, where are you?" and close to my ear Scrapefoot answered, "Here, I've got him!" I gasped for breath before the big hands would make breathing a thing of the past. The sweet barbershop odor was almost overpowering.

The edge of the cutting bench pressed against my back. The hands tightened. Pinwheels of red, yellow and green spun riotously inside my eyeballs. *Jesus, Mary and Joseph,* I thought, *they can hang me up with the rest of the meat . . .*

I brought the maul around in another blind swing, and this time it hit pay dirt. Scrapefoot grunted and his fingers loosened. From the sound of the thud, I think the maul caught him on the side of the neck rather than the head, but it was enough to weaken his grip momentarily.

I kicked out with both feet, and suddenly I was free.

I ducked, twisted and slid along the edge of the bench. My fingers touched the rough masonry of the wall again, and I scuttled along beside it. I could hear my pursuers eight or ten feet away. I held the maul ready in my right hand and kept contact with the wall with my left.

Scrapefoot was closing again. I could smell his barber-shop odor and hear his guttural breathing. I pressed back against the wall as his hands found me—and suddenly the wall gave, and I was stumbling backward in a half-lit room that seemed blindingly bright, with my attacker's fingers clutching my lapels and his ugly face a foot from mine.

I had fallen back through a swinging door that connected the meat storage room with a smaller adjacent room, lit by a small high window. It was apparently used as a storeroom for cheese—great wheels of cheddar were stacked in one corner, and red balls of Edam hung in nets on the walls. Over my shoulder I saw another door at the end of the room and threw myself toward it.

Scrapefoot's fingers remained locked in my lapels. Our momentum carried us across the cheese room and through the second door as though we were flying. We burst through it into the kitchen. It was a room about eighty feet long and, through most of its length, thirty feet wide. But at its extreme end, where I now found myself, it narrowed into a sort of alcove no more than ten feet wide, with double swinging doors in its far wall.

A number of things happened simultaneously as we sailed into the kitchen. A platoon of cooks, assistant cooks, apprentice cooks, bus boys and dishwashers stopped what they were doing in mid-movement and stared at us. Scrape-foot's eyes widened as he realized he was out in the open, and he released his grip and dug in his heels. Freed of his weight, I flew even more swiftly toward the double swinging doors, which opened a moment before I reached them.

A waiter stepped through the doors. His extended hands and arms were concealed under ten or fifteen pounds of dirty dishes—plates and bowls and saucers that overlapped like shingles on a roof. Above them only his nose, eyes and forehead were visible. It is remarkable that such a small facial area could communicate such consternation.

I struck him in the middle of the crockery, and the two of us cartwheeled into the grand dining room.

The explosion of china cut through the conversation and mastication of a thousand diners like a whisper of scandal at a quilting bee. Mouths dropped open to expose gobbets of pheasant, terrapin and *pomme de terre Bonne Jeanne*. Glasses of hock and claret paused in midair, fans ceased to flutter, children interrupted their whining, waiters forgot to sneer. Diners at tables close to the scene stayed riveted in their seats; those at tables immediately behind rose to a half-crouch; those behind them rose to a standing position; the remainder stood on tiptoe and craned their necks.

Plates and saucers continued to crash for four or five seconds after the original detonation.

In the silence that followed the final smash, I opened my eyes and surveyed the disaster. A foot or two away, awash in crockery shards, the waiter lay on his elbows, regarding me with loathing too intense for words. I raised my eyes to the diners at the nearest table—and despair descended like a shroud.

For there, hunched forward over his hamlike fists, his square German face an apoplectic red, sat Police Captain Fred Winklemann.

The first thing I saw in Captain Winklemann's office was the current issue of *The Spirit of the Times*, folded to reveal my—or Hochmuth's—article. Winklemann sat down at his

desk and placed one hand on the newspaper. He regarded
me with the forced patience of a judge listening to a statement from a prisoner he has already decided to hang.
"There's a story here about a naked body being found on
a dumbwaiter in the United States Hotel. There's also a lot
of stuff about underworld figures and confidence games involving important society figures. Did you write the story,
Moretti?"

"No, not really. I—well, some of the facts came from
me, but I didn't mean for them to get printed."

He raised his blond caterpillar eyebrows. "You send
your editor stories that you don't want to get printed?"

"Not as a rule, no. But sometimes—ahh, 'tis hard to
explain to a rational man like yourself, who hasn't been
corrupted by the foolishness of the newspaper business."
I smiled sheepishly.

He was unmoved either by the brogue or the ovine
expression. "I told you what I was going to do to you if
you brought any scandal on Saratoga Springs, didn't I, Moretti?"

"That you did, Captain, that you did. No fairer statement could any man ask, and that's a fact." Idiotically I
seemed unable to stop talking like a bogtrotter from County
Clare. "But since that time an item or two has come to
light that I welcome this opportunity to bring to your attention—"

"What were you doing in the kitchen of the United States
Hotel, and why did you knock down that waiter and smash
all his crockery?"

"That's part of what I want to tell you, Captain," I
continued desperately. "I was attacked by two thugs in the
room where they hang up sides of beef. They were trying
to kill me. 'Twas only by the grace of God I was able to
escape into the kitchen."

"What two men? There were no two men with you when

you charged through the swinging doors and assaulted that waiter."

"They must have gone back through the cheese room, and then on through the beef room, where they were waiting for me to start with."

"And *why* were they waiting for you to start with?"

The questioning was getting out of control and if I wanted to keep Kate Linnett's name out of it—which I did—I had to try to channel Winklemann's curiosity. I raised one hand to request a momentary hiatus. "Captain, believe me, I can understand how you're feeling. I can see how you might be tempted to hold me to blame for the unfortunate news story in the paper there. I think you'd be being unfair, and I know you'll regret it later because you're a fair man at heart, but I can see how you'd be tempted." He started to interrupt but I hurried on: "But without going into all that now, I think I may have a bit of information that may help you solve your murder. Captain, have you ever heard of Frog Robinette?"

He regarded me silently for a moment while he decided whether or not I could be trusted with a simple yes/no answer. Then he answered, "No."

"Frog Robinette is a product of the stews of New Orleans, where he was a member of the infamous Pontchartrain Tigers. After a brief career as a carnival roustabout and performer, he moved on to become a confidence man, working with such leading practitioners as the Foul-Mouthed Kid, Foureyes Mooney and Duke Mindarez. . . ."

"You mean Duke Ramirez?" Winklemann asked.

"Ramirez, yes—Mindarez is one of his aliases." I paused to regain control of the narrative. "Ahh—the point about Ramirez is, he was an expert on a con game called the Spanish Prisoner. Do you know what the Spanish Prisoner is, Captain Winklemann?" Winklemann nodded, lips tightened slightly. "So Frog Robinette also became an expert in working the Spanish Prisoner," I went on. "And Frog Robinette is right here in Saratoga Springs, and you can't walk through Dirty Helen's without hearing somebody whispering about the Spanish Prisoner to somebody else."

"How do you know this Robinette is here at the Springs?"

"Because I saw him. You showed him to me, Captain. He's the corpse you pulled out of the dumbwaiter at the United States Hotel!"

I felt very good about the way I had built to the revelation, in spite of the slight *gaffe* about Duke Ramirez' alias. Winklemann regarded me with frank curiosity. "Assuming what you're saying is not pure unadulterated horse frockey, how do you know about Robinette, and how do you know he's the man under the sheet in the basement?"

I smiled apologetically. "I wish I could tell you, but you know how it is with a reporter's sources."

"Don't give me any crap about sources, you tricky son-of-a-bitch. In about one minute I'm going to have you handcuffed and put on a slow train for Albany. Now I said, how do you know about Robinette?"

I backed water somewhat. "From an old friend of mine who used to be a Pinkerton, Hugh Llewellyn."

Winklemann nodded. "Taffy the Welshman. I should have asked him to come in. If the dead man had a record, Taffy would know him all right. He's got a memory like an encyclopedia." He glared at me. "All right. What else have you got?"

"Gus Gibbons, a crooked tout who's been warned off half the tracks in the country. He's up to his old tricks—I saw him in action the other day."

He dismissed this information with a wave of his meaty hand. "I'm not asking you about touts. I'm asking you about that stuff you had in your story."

"Well, what about those two plug-uglies that jumped me in the meat storeroom?"

"That you *say* jumped you in the meat storeroom," he amended.

"Captain, you don't think I dreamed up this stunt as some kind of Halloween prank! I swear to you that two men attacked me and tried to kill me in there!"

"What were you doing in the meat locker to begin with?"

This time I had an acceptable answer to the question. I adopted the sheepish expression again. "To tell you the truth, after I saw that story in *The Spirit of the Times*, I thought it might be just as well to leave some distance between the two of us. So I've been doing my coming and going through the back storerooms. The two men must have followed me in, and then waited for me to come out again."

"All right, tell me everything you remember about what happened in the meat room."

I described the encounter as completely as I could. Winklemann listened without interruption until I was finished. Then he asked, "That smell you mentioned—you called it a barbershop smell. Try to pin that down."

I shook my head. "I've been trying to, but I can't. You know how it is when a smell reminds you of another place, and all at once you feel like you're there again, but you can't figure out why? That's the way it was with this. Somehow for a moment I was in a barbershop, lying back in the chair with my eyes closed, waiting for something pleasant to happen. . ."

". . . and then the barber splashed the bay rum on you and rubbed it in."

I sat up straight. "That's right! It did smell like bay rum! How did you know that?"

He didn't answer directly. "That name you said one of the men called the other—what did it sound like again?"

I closed my eyes to think. "It might have been Ace, or Jase, or Case. I'm sure it had an 'ase' sound to it."

"How about Face?"

"It could have been Face—except who ever heard of a name like Face?"

Again Winklemann didn't answer. Instead, he regarded me somberly, as if considering my fate. "Moretti," he said finally, "I think you're telling me the truth, which is lucky for you. I'm not sure it's all the truth, but I think it's the truth as far as it goes. Very well. I'm going to let you stay here at the Springs through the end of the meet, as long as you fulfill certain obligations." He numbered them on his square-tipped fingers: "First, no more scandal—not a word. Second, you tell me anything you hear about Frog Robinette and the Spanish Prisoner grift. And don't, I repeat, don't put on any more exhibitions in the grand dining room of the United States Hotel, or anywhere else where more than two people can see you at any one time. Have you got all that?"

"Yes, sir. Was the name I heard Face?"

"Goodbye, Moretti. I hope I don't see you again under unfavorable circumstances."

I walked back to the hotel. It was dark by now, and the orchestra was playing in the garden. Fireflies blinked in the soft perfumed air, and an orange full moon was rising over the east wing. Arm in arm, couples promenaded along the curving walks, the ladies somehow birdlike in their plumed hats, the gentlemen with their canes on their arms and their corporations thrust out before them.

Once again I was persuaded that since I was in Saratoga on an August evening I must be a successful man. Well, why not? Winklemann was letting me stay in town, and I no longer needed to skulk in back hallways and paint myself with burnt cork to avoid detection. Kate Linnett offered two enticing mysteries—the question of Mrs. Murchison's missing $120,000 worth of bearer bonds, and the question of Kate Linnett herself, one or both of which I intended to solve before I left the Springs. *Both, I should think,* I reflected comfortably as I lit a cigar and tasted the first mouthful of pungent smoke.

The music seemed to be a program of Viennese waltzes, and I listened idly for five or ten minutes while my thoughts skipped from one pleasant subject to another. Once or twice the recollection of my near demise in the meat locker intruded, but I resolutely changed the subject. A firefly-spangled Saratoga night was no time for lugubrious thoughts.

When my cigar was halfway down I threw it away and entered the lobby. There was an envelope in my box behind the front desk. A good deal of my euphoria drained away when I saw it was a telegram.

It was from Hochmuth, of course:

PADDY MORETTI, UNITED STATES HOTEL, SARATOGA SPRINGS, N.Y.

YOUR FAITHFUL READERS EAGERLY AWAIT FULL STORY OF MURDER COMMA NOTORIOUS UNDERWORLD FIGURES COMMA BIZARRE SWINDLES STOP AM CONFIDENT YOU WILL NOT DISAPPOINT THEM STOP DUE TO DEMOCRAT IN WHITE HOUSE JOBS NOT EASY TO FIND COMMA ESPECIALLY FOR BLACK-LISTED REPORTERS STOP BEST WISHES

HOCHMUTH

I quickly ran through all my available epithets in English, Gaelic and Italian and was unable to find a single one adequate to describe the man. With unmatched perfidy he had

published my most confidential private message, and now
demanded that I document it on pain of discharge and
blacklisting. I crushed the sheet of flimsy into a ball and
dropped it into the nearest cuspidor.

Once in my miserable room I made myself a drink and
read through the notes I had made since my arrival, hoping
to find a clue I might have missed before, either with regard to the match race or the murder of Robinette. I found
nothing. I leafed through my notebook of sources, hoping
to find someone beside Taffy the Welshman who might
have information to help me. I found no one.

With a sigh I put the papers away and finished my drink.
Then I rinsed out my glass, straightened my tie and made
my way to room 312.

6

Recollections through a Glass, Darkly

I knocked gently on the door and she opened it immediately. "Be very quiet," she whispered as she stepped aside to let me enter. "She's been very uncomfortable all day and I just this minute got her to sleep."

I told her that due to improved relations with the Saratoga Police I could now afford to be seen in public, and asked her to have dinner with me.

She frowned thoughtfully. "Why, I don't know. Theoretically, this *is* my day off, although I can't remember the last time I took advantage of it. And Mrs. Murchison took a sleeping draught and shouldn't wake up for hours. . ."

"Come on, then, and we'll kick up our heels like a couple of foals in a field of Kentucky bluegrass," I urged. She hesitated, then threw a lilac shawl around her shoulders.

I took her to a small restaurant called Mama Sentelli's, which offered the twin advantages of being inexpensive and Italian. We began with antipasto and a Chianti a bit too sour and grainy for the taste of most Americans. She was delighted with it. When the minestrone came she covered it with a layer of Parmesan cheese and sopped it up with bread like any wagoneer in the Abruzzi.

"I like the way you eat," I said.

Her eyes sparkled. "I like to eat," she answered.

Further conversation proved impossible until we had finished our spaghetti and clam sauce. Then, as we lingered over dessert and *espresso*, she said, "Did it bother you, the way I tied into that food?"

"Lord, no. Why would it? I grew up in a family of spaghetti-eaters, remember. We were always hungry, and half of us were girls."

"We were always hungry too, it seems like. I remember we had to wait till Pappa came home from work before we could have supper—he was always back by five-thirty, but it seemed like forever. In the wintertime it would have been dark for an hour. Mamma would be in the kitchen and my little brother and I would be at the table trying to do our lessons by the coal-oil lamp, and all I could think about was food." She laughed and shook her head, and her heavy auburn hair caught reflections in the candlelight. "My recollection of my childhood is twelve years of thinking about food. That's not very genteel, is it?"

It seemed almost unbelieveable to me that this cool, poised and disturbingly attractive woman had grown up worrying about an empty belly. "Well, you're certainly not suffering from malnutrition now," I said impulsively. Her eyebrows rose slightly. "What I mean is, I think you've filled out fine. In the right places, I mean. Not everywhere. You look—very healthy."

She bowed her head gravely. "Thank you. I haven't, always."

"Tell me about your family, and about where you lived in Goshen."

"Oh, it was just a family, just a house. My father worked in the lumberyard. I don't think it was a very good job, none of his jobs were. I don't remember much about that year—just some of the kids at the school." Her eyes looked steadily into mine, and I could almost hear the next (un-spoken) words: *Like you, Paddy Moretti. You're what I remember most.*

"Where did you go after Goshen?"

"There were so many towns, I'm not sure which came first. Peavyville, and Goodis, and Frenchburg, and Fetzer Junction and Canton and Utica and—" She waved one hand helplessly. "You don't care and I don't care, Paddy. The point is, I got away from them. They're so unimportant to me now I can't even remember which order they came in."

"I wish you had stayed in Goshen longer."

She smiled. "So do I." She stirred her coffee, and I noticed that her fingers were long and slender; the nails, however, were clipped almost down to the quick. She sipped from her cup and replaced it in the saucer. "Tell me how you came to venture out into that great world beyond Goshen," she said.

I told her about the various jobs that led me to my pres-ent tenuous connection with *The Spirit of the Times*. She listened attentively, a trace of a smile on her full lips. When I reached a stopping place, she said, "So you got to New York finally. I'm not surprised. I think you were bound to."

"You think New York is all that different from other places?"

"I think New York is—" She hesitated, and her hazel eyes sparkled with remembered excitement. "Have you ever been to Sherry's, Paddy?"

"Sherry's Restaurant? Yes, a few times. Why?"

"I never have. But once, when I'd only been in New York a day or two, I stood on the sidewalk and watched the carriages drive up and the people go in. They were the handsomest men and the most beautiful women I've ever seen. A funny, dumpy little woman standing beside me knew all their names; they were the people you read about in the society section. Lily Langtry was one of them—I remember she came with a tall, good-looking man named Van something, Van Arsdale, Van Ackerman, something like that. Her dress was a kind of shimmery electric blue that seemed to float around her, and her hat looked like it was going to take off and fly away. She had her hand on his arm, and he was holding his hand over it, very possessive, and you just knew that he was madly in love with her and would give her anything in the world if she would just be his and only his—but of course she wouldn't, because she wanted more than any one man could give. . . ."

She paused, eyes wide and lips parted, and I wondered if in memory she had ceased to be Kate Linnett and had become the Jersey Lily, as far beyond selfishness as a Siamese cat is beyond modesty.

I leaned toward her and said, "Some day I'll take you there, Kate."

She seemed not to hear me. "They kept coming in their fine carriages, the beautiful women and the handsome men, and the funny little woman beside me would recognize them and call out their names—'Hurray for Lily Langtry! Hurray for James Van Arsdale!'—and they would nod their heads to us and smile, and their carriages would drive away to wait until they were wanted again.

"It must have been a special party at Sherry's that night, because after an hour or so the guests stopped arriving, and the people in the crowd started drifting away. The funny little woman said, 'Well, dear, it's been lovely, hasn't it?' just as if we'd both been guests at another party, right there on the sidewalk."

"Did you wait to see them come out again?"

"Oh, no." She laughed shortly. "I was a working girl—or at least I hoped to be, if I could find a job the next day—

and working girls can't waste their nights standing outside fancy restaurants. But I never forgot them." She looked at me, unsmiling. "You want to know if New York's different from other places? Show me Sherry's in Goshen, Ohio."

"How about here in Saratoga? The Jersey Lily came here for the races, remember."

"Two weeks a year." She shook her head impatiently. "It's not the same thing." A frown put petulant lines between her eyebrows.

"Well, I'm glad we're here instead of New York tonight," I said, signaling the waiter for the check. "It'll be a lot easier looking for information on Mrs. Murchison's bonds here than it would be there."

I paid the waiter and tipped him more than I normally would have. On the way out I introduced Kate to "Mama Sentelli." He was a slight, swarthy Neapolitan with a crooked spine that made him look hunchbacked, and his name was Joe Palladaglia. He listened expressionlessly to Kate's compliments on the dinner and said, "A thousand thanks, Signorina." His eyes flicked to me. "Everything all right, *paisan?*"

"As always, Joe." I patted my stomach. "If I ate here more than twice a year, I'd be pushing around a belly like Diamond Jim Brady." He smiled sourly; after all, he ate his own pasta every day and couldn't have weighed more than 100 pounds dripping wet.

I lowered my voice. "I need some information, Joe. I'm trying to find out who's been betting more than he has a right to be betting during the last two or three days."

His impatient eyes left mine and moved around the dining room. "I run a restaurant, Paddy, not a handbook."

"I know that. I also know you pick up sixty percent of the gossip in town."

"Sixty-five percent. What are you looking for—some

bank cashier who's embezzled the widows' and orphans' life savings?''

"No, nothing like that. This is somebody in the business, I think. Somebody who follows the races. I could be wrong, but I doubt it.''

Palladaglia continued to inspect his establishment. "All the real advance money is going on the match race.'' he said thoughtfully. "Most of it on The Mogul. If The Mogul wins, nobody's going to make a hell of a lot of money. The odds are too short.''

"But if The Mogul loses—'' I suggested.

"If The Mogul loses, still nobody's going to make a hell of a lot of money, unless they've bet heavy on Tenstrike. And nobody's bet that heavy on Tenstrike. If they had, it would have shown up in the odds.''

That was true. In a two-horse race, any bet that wasn't *on* a horse was *against* that horse. Odds showed an immediate and direct relationship to the money bet.

I thought about it. "You're not saying there's no way for anybody to make a killing on this, are you?''

He looked at me pityingly. "You know better than that, *paison.* All I'm saying is I haven't heard of any particular person setting up for it.''

"All right, Joe. But if you do hear anything, will you let me know?''

"If it's nothing I'll get my throat cut for.''

"Arrivederci, Joe.''

He nodded politely to Kate. *"Arrivederci,* Signorina. Come see us again.''

I hailed a cab outside and helped Kate up the step. "Drive around Congress Spring Park for ten minutes,'' I told the driver. "Then I'll tell you where to go.''

"Why?'' Kate asked simply.

"Because there are some things I have to know if I'm going to be any help to you.''

"I thought I'd already told you everything you wanted to know."

"Not quite." The cab rounded a corner and entered the Broadway evening traffic. It was the time when all the residents of Saratoga feel they are obliged to leave where they are and go some place else, preferably at high speed. As our cabbie skillfully entered the flow, the snort of horses, the creak of wood and leather, the jangle of chains and the curses of the sweating drivers were an engulfing cacophony. A phaeton on our left swung so close its wheels were only an inch from ours; a landau in front of us slowed so suddenly our driver had to tug on the handbrake, almost throwing us from our seat. The driver behind us screamed profanity.

But the incredible part of this was the behavior of the passengers in the cabs and carriages. No matter how close their drivers brought them to destruction, they ignored it entirely, smiling and chatting and flirting as if they were seated on horsechair sofas in some fashionable salon. It was as if they were sealed and insulated in a transparent cocoon called Society, which was inpenetrable to dust and noise and discomfort.

We stayed in Broadway's raging torrent for a minute or two before turning off to circle Congress Spring Park. The driver slowed to a trot and then, when I requested it, to a walk. The residential street was startling quiet.

"Now we can hear ourselves think," I said. "Kate, have you ever known a man called Frog Robinette?"

She frowned. "No, I don't think so. I've never known anybody named Frog. Why? Is it important?"

"He's the man whose body was found in the dumbwaiter at the hotel." I went on to describe his personal appearance. "Does that sound like anybody you've ever seen?"

She shook her head. "I think I'd remember seeing somebody like that."

"Not necessarily. He was an actor, with a lot of experience with make-up. He could have looked like anybody." I thought a minute. "Kate, those séances Mrs. Murchison held—was there anybody who came to them who might have been Robinette in disguise?"

"Very few men ever came, Paddy. Men tend to be suspicious of contact with the Other World—at least, that's what Mrs. M. thinks. And I'm sure the ones who did come were just who they said they were. There wasn't a false mustache in the bunch."

Did Mrs. Murchison ever mention her bonds during these meetings? Or could she have mentioned them privately to any of her—ah, patrons?"

"I don't think so. Mrs. M. is pretty close-mouthed about her personal affairs." My hand was on the seat between us, and impulsively she put her hand on top of it. "Oh, Paddy, you do think there's a chance we can find out something, don't you? I'm afraid that poor woman will never get out of her bed again if we can't do something to help her."

I put one arm around her shoulders and patted the firm flesh of her arm reassuringly. "Put your trust in Moretti," I said.

"Oh, I do," she breathed.

I kissed her, and then kissed her again. I was about to kiss her a third time when the cabbie turned and said apologetically, "Pardon me, sir, but I thought you might want to know there's a cab following us. It turned off Broadway right behind us, and it's stayed there ever since."

I leaned over the side and looked back. A hundred yards away was another cab. In the dark shadows of the elm trees that lined the street, I could barely make out the horse and the silhouetted driver; the passengers, if there were any, were invisible.

Kate clutched my arm. "Who do you think it is?" she asked in a low voice.

"I'm not sure." I tugged on the driver's coattails. "Driver, take us to Dirty Helen's—I mean the Saratoga Chip. And don't let that cab catch us on the way!"

He whipped his horse into a brisk trot, and the driver of the cab behind us followed suit. He did not, however, attempt to catch us, being content to keep the same distance between us until we drew up in front of the gambling club. When we stopped, he also stopped. I helped Kate down, paid the driver and then stood undecided on the sidewalk, trying to make up my mind whether to accost the followers or not. Kate pulled my arm. "Come inside, Paddy. If they don't want to be seen, they won't let you get close enough to see them. And if they do let you get close, they might want to hurt you."

I allowed her to lead me into Dirty Helen's. The memory of my experience in the meat room of the United States Hotel was fresh enough to incline me toward discretion.

Inside, we found the dining room almost empty and the gaming rooms crowded and noisy. Helen Liebowitz, resplendent in an emerald-green brocade gown trimmed with monkey fur and faded by perspiration stains under the arms, spied us as we entered. I introduced her to Kate and asked her to have a glass of champagne with us. She shrugged. "If you're buying, what the hell. I've got a thirst like a camel, so watch out." She led the way to an empty table in the dining room and shouted our order to a nearby waiter.

I asked her the same question I'd asked Joe Palladaglia, and which I expected to ask twenty or thirty other people before the night was through. She frowned and snapped a crimson fingernail against her teeth.

"Somebody who's been betting more than he has a right to be betting? No—but that doesn't mean anything, because I'm too busy watching the store to pay much attention to the ponies. Hell, I haven't even been out to the track this season.''

"Well, how about here at the club, or at one of the other clubs? Has anybody been plunging with a bigger roll than you'd expect him to carry? Some nickel-and-dimer, maybe, laying the geetus out at the roulette table or playing in a no-limit poker game?''

"Not that I've noticed." The waiter appeared with the champagne and poured us each a glass. Dirty Helen tasted hers and pursed her mouth in distaste. Then she shrugged. "What the hell, they don't come here for the bubbly anyway.''

She was right about the champagne. I tasted it and set my glass aside. "What about a con man named Frog Robinette? Does that name ring any bells?" She shook her head. "He used to play a game called the Spanish Prisoner," I added.

"Wait a minute. Seems like I heard somebody mention the Prisoner just lately. Somebody talking at the bar." She creased her forehead as she attempted to flesh out the recollection, then shook her head. "No, it's gone."

"Are you sure?" I described Robinette's physical appearance. "Could it have been him?''

"Could have been. I just don't remember."

"Do you remember who he was talking to?''

"No, I got no picture of it at all. Only that somebody mentioned the Spanish Prisoner. I remember I was surprised; that dodge has whiskers on it down to the floor.''

I sighed and took another sip of my champagne. It hadn't improved. "Helen, have you picked up anything that might make you think it wasn't on the square?''

She started to speak, then stopped, then started again. "No, I can't say there is. Not really."

"What did you start to say, before you changed your mind?" I asked quickly.

"Nothing. I mean, there isn't anything you can put your finger on. Just some little things that don't smell exactly right."

"Like what?"

"Well, like people talking about it who stop talking when you get close to them, like there was something they didn't want you to hear."

"Who, for instance?"

"The Dunne brothers, and that jockey of theirs, Jackie McCandless. I'm sure they were talking about the race the last time they were here, but they shut up as tight as three quahogs when I came over. Then a little while later your friend Sharples came in and sat down with them. They didn't seem to like it very much. He looked like he was asking them questions they didn't want to answer. Finally that little rat McCandless yells 'You keep sticking your nose in things that don't concern you and you're going to get it cut off!' He looked like he was about to pop Sharples one, but old Fergus Dunne cooled him down, and then Sharples left."

I glanced at Kate. She was listening intently, her head resting on her right fist and her hazel-green eyes bright. I said, "Did you hear any of the questions Sharples was asking?"

Helen shook her head. "I was at the other end of the room by then."

"Who else stops talking about the race when you get close to them?"

"Well, some of the touts and bookmakers seem to be more careful than usual. I remember one of them, a fat grafter named Gus Gibbons, shut up right in the middle of a sentence when he saw me sit down at the next table. If I ever saw anybody look guilty, and I've seen a hell of a lot, that Gibbons was one."

"Gibbons—that's interesting. I know the man, I'm sorry

to say. I know what you mean about him looking guilty. Unfortunately, he always looks that way.''

"You're right.'' She emptied her glass and refilled it. "Anybody else?'' Kate and I both shook our heads, and she returned the bottle to its bucket. She drained her glass and put her palms flat on the table. "I've got to move around. Why don't you two try your luck at the tables? This just might be your lucky night.''

"Maybe we will,'' I said. "If you think of anything that might help me, let me know.''

She nodded and left the table. Kate said, "Would she tell you everything she knows?''

I laughed. "Dirty Helen wouldn't tell her confessor everything she knows. But I don't think she'd hold out unless she had a reason. Of course, she may have a reason. Now, unless you want some more of this carbonated dishwater, I suggest we move into the gaming room.''

We stayed at Dirty Helen's for forty-five minutes or so, and I talked to six or seven people I knew while Kate listened unobtrusively at my side. The talking made my throat dry, and I assuaged the discomfort with three tall glasses of Irish whiskey and water. None of the people I talked to could think of anyone who had been betting more than he had a right to bet.

I had just ordered a fourth Irish when Kate said, "Paddy, I've got to get back to my room. It's been almost three hours since we left.''

I glanced at her in surprise. My first feeling was one of disappointment. "Oh, pshaw! It's the shank of the evenin', and all!'' I cried. Then slowly the realization came that I would be taking Kate back to the delicious privacy of her hotel room, where horizons might well be unlimited. "But of course you have to go! What a terrible thing if the poor old woman was to wake up, and you not there to minister to her misery!'' I said emotionally.

We took another cab back to the hotel. I glanced back once, but didn't see any sign of a follower. After that I didn't think to look again.

Kate let us into room 312 and closed the door softly behind her. I reached out my arms but she slipped away from them. "Let me check on Mrs. M.," she whispered, opening the connecting door and disappearing through it.

I paced the available floor space for two or three minutes until she returned. She closed the door quietly behind her and stepped up to me, tilting her face up to mine. Her eyes sparkled, as if from the expectation of imminent happiness, I thought. We kissed, lingeringly. Her mouth was cool and fresh for the first few minutes, and her fingers rested lightly on my shoulders. Then my excitement kindled hers, and her fingers tensed and bored into my muscles. Her mouth opened, her tongue danced with mine, her hips rolled and her firm thigh slipped between my legs.

Ah, Paddy, Paddy, its going to happen, it was meant to be! my blood cried out. Bending, I whipped one arm behind her knees and swept her into the air. "Macushla!" I whispered hoarsely as I carried her to the bed.

When I set her down, the bedsprings shrieked like a wounded shoat. She sat up suddenly just as I was lying down beside her and our foreheads met with a resounding crack. I recoiled, lost my balance on the bed and slid to the floor with a dull thud. When I rose again, it was to find her listening intently, an expression of deep concern on her lovely face.

"It's Mrs. M.!" she whispered. "She must have heard us! I've got to go to her!"

" 'Twas the singing in my heart you heard," I suggested hoarsely as I struggled up over the edge of the mattress.

She pushed past me and stood up. "No, no, it was Mrs. M. I'm sure it was."

She headed for the connecting door. I rolled into a sitting

position. "Damn Mrs. M.!" I hissed. "I think you're making the woman up! Every time I get my arms around you, it's 'Oops, excuse me please, there's Mrs. M. again!' Why don't *I* ever hear her, that's what I want to know!"

"Perhaps it's because you aren't listening." She reached out and took my hand, drawing me after her. "Be very quiet now, doubting Thomas." She stepped noiselessly to the connecting door and opened it. "See?" she whispered. Then she stepped into the adjoining room and closed the door behind her.

During the second or two when I was able to look over her shoulder, I saw a large and well-furnished room with a canopied bed along the far wall. The room was dimly lit by a bedside lamp with its wick turned down. In the shadows beyond the lamp I could make out the outline of a small figure in the bed. At least Mrs. Murchison wasn't sitting up and demanding to be read to, I thought.

When Kate came back, she was brisk and businesslike. "She wasn't awake, but she was restless. I think you'd better go, Paddy. When she's like this, she could wake up any minute."

"I can be very, very quiet," I suggested hopefully.

"No, it wouldn't work. What you better do is go back to those gambling places of yours and try to find out something about our bonds."

"But—" I began.

"Now go!" she commanded. She took some of the peremptoriness out of it by kissing me quickly on the cheek, and them propelled me gently and efficiently through the door. In less time than it takes to describe it, I was standing on the familiar corridor carpet.

What I have to narrate now will be a good deal less than satisfactory. I apologize. When I began this narrative, I promised to tell the literal and exact truth, whether it made me sound like a Pre-Raphaelite poet or an abandoned sensualist. Up to now, I have kept my word. But in describing what follows, I must admit I don't know what the truth is. I have no more clear idea of what occurred than you, the reader, will, if—forewarned by this apologia—you nevertheless follow me through the events of this impenetrable evening.

The next hour or two are clear enough, if a little blurred around the edges. My first feeling on finding myself in the hall outside Kate's door was a dull ache in my lower abdomen—gentlemen will recognize the symptom. Swearing to myself in pain and mortification, I made my way to the grand staircase and descended into the lobby. My thoughts were chaotic. Swift images of Kate were succeeded by recollections of Frog Robinette on his slab, of a tree-shadowed cab waiting like Charon's bark in a darkened road, of glowering Captain Winklemann and lonely Taffy the Welshman, of copper-colored, fastidious Isaac Murphy and venomous porcine Gus Gibbons. And adding urgency to the program, like the ticking of a death-house clock, I remembered the sinister irony of Hochmuth's telegrams.

The situation called for pursuing my investigation and restoring the inner man, both as soon as possible. I took a cab to Donahue's, a casino one peg above Dirty Helen's. I didn't know the manager well enough to pump him, so I went directly to the bar. Three newspapermen I knew were arguing about something at the far end of the room, and I joined them. "Move over, you ink-stained wretches, and let a man get a drink, can't you?" I said by way of greeting.

"If it isn't the Moretti himself." said Samuels of the *World,* a disheartened-looking man with red-rimmed eyes, a boneless nose and almost no shoulders at all. "Taking time off from your criminological pursuits, Paddy?"

"Tell us about the notorious underworld figures and the

bizarre swindles staged against a darkening background of murder,'' said fat, cherub-faced Tallboy of the *Herald*.

"May I have your autograph?" asked smart-alecky Ackerman of the *Tribune*, hooking spatulate thumbs in the armholes of a vest patterned with racehorses. I laughed artificially and ordered a double Irish and water. I drank half of it before answering. "As I see all of you are aware, I am in close pursuit of a story which, in its startling ramifications and revelations of evil, may hereafter be judged as the crime of the decade—perhaps, if you don't count the Hayes-Tilden election, even the crime of the century. Whether or not any or all of you unsuccessful scriveners share modestly in that story depends entirely upon you." I drank the second half of my drink and ordered another.

"A man can't walk on one leg," said Samuels, signaling to the bartender.

"You mean a cockroach can't walk on five legs, don't you?" said Tallboy, also holding up a finger.

"How many does it take a caterpillar?" asked Ackerman, joining his companions.

The drinks arrived. I raised mine in a toast. "Here's to crime, and higher circulation figures." We drank to that. "Now, gentlemen, I want to ask you one simple question."

We began our game for four players. The chips were information, and I was banker, because I knew more, or was believed to know more, about the murder of Frog Robinette than my colleagues. By my questions, Samuels, Tallboy and Ackerman suspected that they might also hold chips, but they were unable to gauge their worth without knowing the chips I held. We all had the same strategy— to find out what the others knew while preserving the exclusivity of our own information.

While we played, we drank.

In retrospect, I believe I won the game. In exchange for

almost no information of my own (I think) I learned that: Harrison Fowler, owner of The Mogul, had hopes of being appointed ambassador to a European country, once the Republicans were back in office; the Dunne brothers were under investigation by a blue-ribbon grand jury in New York City for bucket-shop operations; their jockey, Jackie McCandless, was believed by many knowledgeable racing enthusiasts to have "thrown" at least three races within the past few months; a ring of New York City gamblers was pressing the city of Saratoga Springs to allow more public gambling, appealing to patrons of more modest means; the yearly attempt to open a high-class bordello in the Springs had again been tried this year, and had again failed; Harrison Fowler was believed to have his mistress with him in town, and Fergus Dunne was believed to prefer local boys; a Texan named Clint Maroon had won thirty thousand dollars in a no-limit poker game the night before.

The extraction of this generally inconsequential data from my colleagues took the better part of an hour, during which I continued to restore the inner man. By the end of that time the inner man and the rest of me were both drunk. (I hate the baldness of that word, but sometimes it's better to tell the truth and shame the devil.) The last coherent speech I can remember from that evening came from Samuels of the *World*, as he and his two friends were leaving me to my fate: "And by the way, Moretti. I don't mind you tying up the telegraph at the station for two hours at a time, but kindly stop sending your friend Gus Gibbons there to tie it up for another two hours. After all, fair's fair."

I think I looked at him owlishly and said, "Only reason I'd send Gus Gibbons to the station would be if I knew he'd catch buboes there. Or be hit by falling rocks."

"Well, he said he was sending out some stuff for you, that's all I know."

They left, and I ordered another drink. The bartender

looked dubious, but served it to me. I thought to myself, *Why would Gus Gibbons send telegrams for two hours? Why would he tell another newspaperman he was working for me? Take the second question first, it's easier. Answer, simple malice, hoping to make trouble for me with other newspapermen. Typical of the stupid meanness of the man.*

But why would he send any telegrams at all? To the best of my knowledge Gibbons was barely literate. I puzzled over the question as I finished my drink.

That's all I remember of the bar of Donahue's. The dark shades draw across my memory at that point, only parting to allow glimpses of random and unconnected scenes that stand out like lighted tableaux in a darkened theater.

One scene is a painting on a wall, perhaps in the casino of Donahue's, perhaps somewhere else. It's a copy of a picture I've seen before, a spooky, dreamlike composition called, if I remember correctly, "Death on a Pale Horse." It shows a racetrack at night, muffled in dirty brown-gray darkness. The track is deserted except for a single horse and rider galloping around a turn in the middle distance. The horse is scrawny and its color is the color of phlegm. The rider is a skeleton, carrying a scythe in bony fingers. A snake writhes along the bottom of the canvas. The picture communicates an almost palpable sense of terror, and seems to carry with it the chilly silence of the tomb.

As I struggle to remember that evening, this picture merges into another, whose subject also involves race-horses. It is the climax of the dream I had shortly after I arrived in Saratoga: I am riding a chestnut filly, nearing the end of a race, and suddenly there is Kate, standing beneath a parasol beside the guardrail, cool and calm amid the cheering crowd. Then the horse breaks down and starts to fall, her head strikes the dirt, and she cartwheels, pinning me beneath her heaving body as Kate smiles gently from behind the fence . . .

Another scene from memory, this time accompanied by a smell: I am in a crowd of people. I am being jostled and shoved, perhaps due to my own clumsiness. It is indoors, and many of the men around me are in evening clothes, so I know I am at a casino. I have a few bills in my hand. I wish to place a bet on the roulette board, but can't get close enough to the table to put my money down. As I struggle through the crowd, I suddenly smell the cloying odor of bay rum. My body turns to ice. My instinct urges me to flee, but the press of bodies around me prevents it. I look over my shoulder, and there, not a foot behind me, is the heavy face, the tiny asymmetrical eyes and flattened nose, the gold tooth glittering between slack lips, of the man I think of as Scrapefoot. I redouble my efforts to escape, but the wall of flesh around me is immovable . . .

I have a memory of Sharples, my colleague and competitor from *The Thoroughbred Record*. Somewhere the two of us are sitting together, drinking, and Sharples is laughing at me. "You damned fool," he says, "when you want to find money, you go where the money is!"

"And where's that?" I asked.

"Where it always is. The trick's not finding it, the trick's getting away with some for yourself."

I shake my head stupidly, trying to put my senses in order. "I don't understand," I mumble.

"You will," he says, grinning. "You just keep your eye on your Uncle Dudley."

I remember the smell and taste of wet fog on my face, and the *clop, clop* of a horse's hoofs on cobblestone. I am sprawled across the seat of an open cab, and the black foliage of trees blots out the sky above me. I am entirely disoriented, having no idea what I am doing in the car or where it is taking me. I consider asking the cabbie, but reject the idea. *Mustn't let him think I'm drunk,* I tell myself. I close my eyes.

And finally I remember a terrible face gazing sightlessly up at me from the floor—eyes bulging, unfocused, lips purple, mouth twisted in an agonized caricature of laughter. The fat neck is stretched taut, and sausage-shaped fingers clutch motionlessly at a swollen belly under a blood-drenched shirt.

Unlike the other memory tableaux, this one did not end. For I was awake now, standing in Gus Gibbons' room, and bright daylight was streaming in through the windows. At my feet lay Gibbons, with a bloody kitchen knife by his side and a mortal wound in his guts. And I had not the faintest idea how I had gotten there or what had transpired once I had arrived.

My stomach heaved, and I stumbled across the room to a chipped enameled wash basin in the corner. I couldn't throw up; even with my fingers down my throat, all I could evoke was a drizzle of bitter slime. I gagged and sank to my knees with my forehead pressing the edge of the basin.

When my stomach settled down I stood up and splashed water on my face and wiped myself dry with a dirty towel. Then I turned back to the body on the floor.

Gibbons had died, apparently, from a single deep knife-thrust in the lower abdomen. Judging from the length of the rip in his shirt, the knife had been sawed upward two or three inches after its original placement. His flesh was cooler than normal, but not by much, and there was no apparent rigor in his joints.

I looked around the room quickly. It was completely unfamiliar to me; as far as I could tell, I had never seen it before this moment. It was the kind of room I'd expect Gus Gibbons to live in—small, and made smaller by the slant of the roof along one side, with gaudy floral wallpaper and a painted floor. The only items of furniture were a bed with a brass bedstead and a sagging mattress, a cheap pine armchair, the washstand in the corner and a dresser. On the dresser was a small pile of personal items.

They included a billfold with loose stiching, a key-ring with six keys, an ivory toothpick and a dog-eared slip of paper bearing the message "Trix—after 8—1923 N. Cdr." I looked through the wallet. It contained, in addition to a photograph of a stern-looking old woman with walleyes, a neatly rolled sanitary device and thirty-two dollars in notes, a folded sheet of paper. I unfolded it and saw the following:

✓ A1	✓ LA7
✓ BA2	✓ M3
✓ BO5	✓ NO15
✓ CH15	✓ NY15
✓ C12	OK1
✓ CL4	OM2
✓ D5	PH10
✓ G1	P13
✓ I2	PR3
✓ K5	SF7
✓ L2	SL10

I looked at it blankly. At first glance I had the impression of a list of chemical abbreviations—valences was the word I remembered from somewhere. But why would Gus Gibbons be carrying a list of valences in his billfold, and why would some of them be checked off and some not?

And why are you standing around like a hat-rack, with a body lying dead at your feet? There's been a murder committed here, my boyo! The realization of the dreadful situation I was in flooded over me. Gibbons was dead, murdered sometime during the night, apparently. I was alone with his corpse. Many people knew of my feud with

him, including a number of newspapermen currently in
Saratoga. I had mentioned him to Captain Winklemann. If
I remembered correctly, his name had come up in the conversation at Donahue's, just before the dark curtain had
descended upon my memory. If I had an alibi for the time
of his death, I had no idea what it was. And, with no
explanation to offer for my presence here, I was alone with
his stiffening cadaver.

The only thing that could make my position worse would
be to be found here by the police.

But of course I couldn't just walk away from the body.
Aside from any considerations of morality, civic respon-
sibility, etc., there was the possibility that I would be seen
leaving. Also that some unknown witness could place me
at the scene of the crime. I couldn't chance that—having
the police know I had left the scene of the crime would be
worse than being found there.

There was no help for it. I would have to go to police
headquarters and make a report.

Replacing the list in the billfold, I took one more hasty
look around the room. The bed was unmade, but the crumpled sheets and pillows were concealed beneath a bed-
spread. A cheap carpetbag containing clean shirts and
underclothing was under the bed, and a few ordinary toilet
articles were on a shelf by the washstand. A cigar butt was
in an ashtray. It didn't seem much to leave behind at the
end of a lifetime, even for someone like Gus Gibbons.

I let myself out of the room into a dark, quiet hallway,
and then out of it into the sunshine. The number on the
porch roof was 317, and the street sign at the nearest corner
said "Asbury." I asked a little girl in a swing which way
downtown was, and she pointed the way, not speaking because her mother had warned her not to talk to strangers,
no doubt. Wise mother.

I walked to the Police Station. Captain Winklemann was

in his office. I pushed the door and entered, unannounced. "Captain, I've come here to report a murder," I said.

He looked up with a frown. "Well, you're a little late," he said dryly. "We've had the body in the morgue for the past two hours."

"Body? What body?" I stared at him open-mouthed. "Who in the world are you talking about?"

"Why, your fellow journalist Sharples, who do you think? Somebody beat him to death with a pair of brass knuckles about two o'clock this morning."

7

Winklemann at Work

"**O**h." I didn't say anything more for a few seconds. Then, because nothing better occurred to me I said meekly, "Well, that wasn't exactly the murder I had in mind."

Winklemann didn't like the idea of me bringing him news of a homicide—I had anticipated that. But he *particularly* didn't like the idea of me bringing him news of one homicide while he was still digesting the news of another. The fact that both victims were known to me incensed him even more.

Accompanied by two uniformed policemen, we proceeded immediately to 317 Asbury Street. A middle-aged woman met us on the front porch. Hiding behind her skirt was the little girl I had seen on the swing. The woman said, "Officer, there's been a terrible thing happened—" and the little girl shrieked, "Mama, mama, that's the man!" and pointed a grubby finger at me.

"She was in the yard when I came out, not more than fifteen minutes ago," I told Winklemann nervously.

He looked at me coldly. "Jarvis, stay down here and get this lady's story," he told one of the policemen. "Also the kid's. Then see if there's anybody else in the house who knows anything about a killing last night.''

Winklemann, the other constable and I went up the stairs to Gibbon's room. It was just as I had left it. Gus Gibbons still stared at the ceiling and clawed motionlessly at his ripped belly. The kitchen knife lay at his side, blood darkening on the blade, and a fly buzzed as it circled in the sunlight that poured through the window.

Winklemann checked the body perfunctorily. ''Dead as Kelsey's nuts, all right. I'd say he got himself gutted five or six hours ago. Does that jibe with your recollections, Moretti?''

''I don't have any recollections, Captain, that's the hell of it. I can't remember a thing from the time I was having a few drinks at the bar in Donahue's until I found myself here staring down at the body.''

''Nothing at all, huh? That makes it convenient for the murderer, doesn't it?'' He rose to his feet and dusted off his knees. ''Particularly if you're the murderer.''

''Holy Mother, if I were the murderer do you think I would have broken my neck running to Police Headquarters to report it?'' I cried.

''I don't know, Moretti. Deep thinkers like you baffle me.'' He stepped over to the dresser and inspected the little pile of personal belongings there. ''I suppose you've pawed through this stuff, but for your sake I hope you haven't taken anything.''

I assured him I hadn't. He pushed the keys and the toothpick to one side and inspected the wallet. When he found the folded paper, he unfolded it and smoothed it out on the dresser top. ''Did you see this?'' he asked me. I said I had, but couldn't make head or tail of it. ''No?'' he asked, raising his caterpillar eyebrows. He folded the paper and stuffed it into his coat pocket, carefully rebuttoning the pocket afterward.

For the next ten minutes Captain Winklemann went over Gibbons' room. The man certainly knew his job. When he was finished I was sure nothing had been concealed there. Winklemann grunted and wiped his hands on his pants. "Stay here until the meat wagon comes, Muller," he told the constable. "Then bring all the fellow's personal stuff back with you to the station. Moretti, let's you and me go back to my office for a nice long chat."

On the way back I asked him to tell me about Sharples. "I'll do better than that—I'll show him to you," he said. "You haven't been down to the morgue for a few days. It'll be a treat for you."

Sharples presented an even more upsetting appearance than Gibbons had. For one thing, we had been, if not friends, at least colleagues and drinking companions, and Death seems more formidable when it inhabits familiar flesh. For another thing, the manner of his passing had left its painful mark upon his face.

For Sharples had been beaten to death. His features looked as if they had been made of rubber and then twisted grotesquely out of shape. One cheek bone was collapsed, his nose was bent and flattened and his jaw pushed forward and to the right, exposing the lower teeth. His skin was torn along the outer edge of one eye, so the eye looked as if it could be lifted from the socket like an egg from an egg-cup. His livid coloring was darkened by purple splotches of subcutaneous bleeding, and there were raw abrasions from his hairline to beneath his chin.

I stared in horror and pity. Captain Winklemann said, "It's remarkable what you can do with a pair of brass knuckles when you set your mind to it."

"Poor Sharples. He was a good reporter," I said softly. I couldn't think of anything else to say about him. "Brass knuckles. Sharples wouldn't have a chance against brass knuckles."

"Oh, he put up the best fight he could," Winklemann said, flipping the sheet down to expose the corpse's naked chest and abdomen. He raised one of Sharples' hands and beckoned me to inspect it. "Look under the fingernails. See that?" There were tiny skin-colored wads under each nail. "He left some good scratches on whoever did it, you can bet on that."

I drew one of the cold hands close to my nose and sniffed. There was a faint but unmistakable scent of bay rum. I glanced up at Winklemann to find him watching me sardonically. "Yeah, I noticed," he said. "Maybe it ain't quite time for the mayor to kick me out and give you my job."

"The man who killed him—it has to be the same one who almost got me in the meat room," I said unnecessarily. Winklemann didn't bother to answer. Instead, he pulled the sheet up over Sharples' face, then led the way out of the morgue and up to his office.

He didn't speak until he was seated behind his desk, and I was sitting across from him. Then he said deliberately, "Moretti, I want you to get something straight. The other day I told you that if you gave me any trouble I'd have you on a slow train to Albany before you could say *Schweinsrippchen*. Well, that's changed now. We're not talking about bouncing some nosy reporter out of town. We're talking about Sing Sing. This is a triple murder now, and from where I sit you're up to your ears in it. So you play ball with me, and I mean all the way, or I'll have you up on charges of withholding evidence and accomplice to murder."

I swallowed and answered earnestly. "If it's complete and total cooperation you're looking for, Captain, you need look no farther. Paddy Moretti and *The Spirit of the Times* are in your corner one hundred percent."

"All right, we'll see. First, I want to know every single

thing you can remember about last night. Every detail. Don't leave anything out, no matter how trivial it may seem.''

I thought back over the black moat of forgetfulness to the memories before.

"Well, to begin with, we had dinner at Mama Sentelli's—''

"Wait a minute. Who's 'we'?''

"Oh, just a girl I met at the hotel. Her name's Kate Linnett. She's sort of a nurse-companion for an old crippled lady.'' I answered the question with careful casualness and immediately went on with my account. "Then after dinner we took a cab to Dirty Helen's. On the way I noticed we were being followed.''

"How'd you happen to notice that?''

"Well, to tell you the truth now, I'd had the driver pull off into a quiet side street for a minute or two. The other cab pulled off behind us. It was the driver who called it to my attention.''

"I see.'' Winklemann's hard eyes searched my face. "This other cab—did it try to catch up to you?''

"No sir, it didn't. It kept the same distance behind us all the way to Dirty Helen's.''

"Did you see who was in it?''

I shook my head. "It was too far back, and too dark. All I could see was the silhouette of the driver.''

"All right. Go on,'' Winklemann said.

I told him that we had split a bottle of champagne with Helen Liebowitz, and then spent forty-five minutes or so in the gaming room. During that time I had seen half a dozen people I knew and had spoken to them. Then I took Kate back to the hotel.

"Straight back, or by way of some more quiet side streets?'' Winklemann asked.

"Straight back,'' I answered.

"Anybody follow you this time?"

"I have no idea. I didn't look back."

"All right, so you took her back to the hotel. Whose room did you go to, hers or yours?"

"Captain—" I began indignantly, then stopped at the look in his small cold eyes. "Her room," I said in a small voice.

"How long did you stay there?"

"Not more than five minutes—just long enough to say goodbye. It's the God's truth, Captain—in five minutes by the clock I was standing in the hall outside her door." *And wishing I had a hundred-pound barbell to lift,* I added to myself.

"Humph," he said obscurely. He picked up a pencil and tapped the point on the desk in front of him. After three taps it broke, and he tossed the pencil away. "After you took her to her room, then what?"

"I took a hack to Donahue's. There were three newspapermen I knew in the bar—" I mentioned their names and the papers they worked for—"and we talked shop and had a few drinks. Well, more than a few drinks. It's here that my memory starts to go bad."

"Just do the best you can, Moretti."

I closed my eyes and thought. "We talked about the murder at the hotel, but none of them knew any more about it than I did. We went over a lot of racetrack gossip about Harrison Fowler and the Dunne brothers and Jackie McCandless. . ." Winklemann interrupted to ask for specifics, and I told him everything I could remember. "After that the three of them went away," I continued. "But the last thing Samuels said was that Gus Gibbons had tied up the telegraph at the railroad station for two hours. I remember that surprised me; I never thought of him as the literary type."

The office door opened and the constable named Muller stuck his head in. "Got that body here now, Captain."

"Stick him down in the basement beside the others," Winklemann directed. "If this keeps up, we're going to have to rent more space. Hire a hall, maybe." Muller withdrew. Winklemann looked thoughtfully at me. "You say Gibbons tied up the telegraph for two hours?"

"That's what Samuels said, Captain."

"Yeah." He unbuttoned his coat pocket and withdrew the folded sheet of paper he had taken from Gus Gibbons' billfold. He didn't unfold it, but tapped its edge against his desk. "All right, what happened then?"

I shrugged my shoulders. "I'm at the end of me tether," I said with a plaintive smile. "That's the last clear recollection I've got until I found myself in Gibbons' room this morning."

"Look, Moretti, don't make me keep reminding you that you're in bad, bad trouble. You've got eight or ten hours to account for, and if you can't do it, you're a number one candidate for the big house on the Hudson. Now think about that, and start remembering."

I did the best I could. He identified the picture of "Death on a Pale Horse" from my description of it. "Yeah, I've seen it. It's in Donahue's game room, on the far wall by the service bar. How come you remember that?" I told him I had no idea. He waved me on. I described my discovery of Scrapefoot close behind me at the roulette table, and the sudden smell of bay rum. He leaned forward. "What did he look like?" he demanded.

"A heavy, meaty face, little crooked eyes, a flat nose like a boxer's, and a gold tooth that caught the light—a real plug-ugly."

He nodded. "That's Face, all right. Go on."

"Captain, isn't it time that *you* told *me* a couple of things—"

"No. Go on."

I told him about talking to Sharples, quoting the three or four sentences I could remember. He made me repeat them twice. " 'When you want to find money,' " he mused, " 'you go where the money is.' No, I don't guess anybody would argue with that, would they?" I said I certainly wouldn't.

I told him about driving through the wet fog in an open cab. "It was at night, but I don't know how late. I was alone, and I was going somewhere, not just riding around."

"Did you notice if anybody was following you then?"

I was tempted to claim I had noticed a follower in order to provide Winklemann with another murder suspect. As I hesitated I glanced at the set of his jaw. "No, Captain, I didn't," I admitted—and then added hopefully, "But that doesn't mean there couldn't have been somebody back there!"

"All right, you went somewhere in a hack. Then what?"

"That's the end of it. The next thing I remember is morning, and Gibbons dead on the floor."

Winklemann frowned. "Try to think, Moretti. This is important. Can you remember going up the stairs? Knocking on the door? Somebody letting you in? Can you remember any faces, any voices, any smells? Eating anything, or drinking anything? Was there any argument, anybody yelling or cussing? Any kind of a fight, somebody pushing somebody, hitting somebody, calling for help? Can you remember seeing some money? Or a knife?"

All through his catechism I shook my head dumbly. When he finished I said, "I'm sorry."

Winklemann sighed and tilted back in his chair. "Sometime between eleven and twelve o'clock last night your friend Sharples got himself beaten to death. His body was found about a mile outside of town under a clump of trees on the road to the track. He may have been killed there—

or he may have been killed somewhere else and dumped there—we can't tell for sure. You smelled his fingers, so you've got a pretty good idea who killed him. The fellow you call Scrapefoot; his real name's Face Hogan. He's a professional bully-boy who likes to work with brass knuckles. As far as I know he's never killed anybody before, but there's always a first time."

"You knew who he was the first time I mentioned him, didn't you?"

"Maybe I had an idea. He's been in town before, doing jobs for one person or another." He paused, then went on: "The Dunne brothers, among others."

I felt a surge of excitement. "You think he's working for them now, Captain?"

"I'll ask him when I find him."

"You know, there were two of them after me in the hotel meat room. Maybe the other fellow worked with him when he killed Sharples, too."

"Maybe." Winklemann seemed to have lost interest in the subject. He unfolded the sheet of paper from Gibbons' billfold and studied it a moment, then handed it across the desk to me. "Look this over. Take your time. Tell me what you see."

I ran down the list of capital letters and numbers slowly. "It's in alphabetical order . . . it's not a bunch of chemical valences, like I thought at first . . . the first two-thirds or so have been checked off, but the rest haven't. . ." I was aware of Winklemann's fingers drumming impatiently on the desk top. "The highest number is fifteen, and there are only three of them. . ." I was silent a few seconds as I studied the numbers. Three times fifteen was forty-five, two times the next largest number, ten, was twenty . . . without any sense of direction, I found myself adding all the numbers together.

The sum was 120.

Carefully I added them up again. They still totaled 120. *Watch out*, I told myself. *Remember Winklemann's never heard of any missing bearer bonds. Anyway, it's probably just a coincidence.* But of course I didn't think it was. I raised my head and said humbly, "It's a great mystery to me, Captain."

"Look at the three items with the biggest numbers—the ones with the fifteens beside them. What are they?"

"CH, NO AND NY," I answered.

"CH, NO and NY. Does that suggest something to you? Use your head, Moretti!"

I stared at each of the three double initials. "No, I'm sorry, Captain. All I can think of is that NO means No, and NY is the abbreviation for New York. . ." I ran my eye over the list, checking for other state abbreviations. The only possibilities were the single letters A, C, D, G, K, L, M, and P. I looked up helplessly.

Winklemann glared at me like an animal trainer running out of patience with a particularly obtuse four-footed student. "And is New York *only* the name of a state?" he demanded.

"Why, no, It's the name of a city, too—" I stopped and looked back at the paper. Of course. I felt like five kinds of fool. "—and NO is New Orleans, and CH is Chicago—"

Winklemann came around the desk and took the list from my hand. "—and BA is Baltimore, BO is Boston, CI and CL are Cincinnati and Cleveland, PH and PI are Philadelphia and Pittsburgh. The tip-off is the double letters-the single letters could stand for anything. But when you see LA and SF and SL, you know you must be talking about cities."

"You think the single letters stand for cities too?"

"Sure—cities that you don't need two letters to identify. There's only one big city in the country that begins with

A: Atlanta. So one letter is enough to identify it. But P might be Philadelphia *or* Pittsburgh, so you use two letters to make sure. This is a list of cities, Moretti—you can bank on it.''

"What about the numbers after them?''

Winklemann put his hands over his kidneys and stretched his back. "Got up too damn early this morning, pulling in corpses. Think I'll go home and take a nap after lunch.'' He went back to his chair and sat down. "I'd guess they stand for money, probably in thousands of dollars. So now we know what Gibbons was doing at the telegraph station.''

"Layoff money?'' I asked. "He was hedging his bets?''

"Maybe. I don't think so, though. Gibbons wasn't big enough to book bets that big—there's over a hundred thousand dollars there, if we've figured it right. I don't think he was laying off—I think he was placing the bets himself, acting for somebody else. I think he was working from this list somebody gave him, or he may have made it himself, telegraphing people he knew all across the country and having them place bets for him locally. He checked off each city when he placed a bet. He'd worked himself down as far as New York City, and probably expected to finish up today.

"Now here's a question for a smart newspaperman, Moretti. Why would anybody want to place out-of-town bets by telegraph when there are two hundred more or less reputable bookmakers in Saratoga Springs?''

Remembering Joe Palladaglia's comments on the advance betting for the match race, I was ready with an answer. "Because it's the only way to get heavy money down on Tenstrike without changing the odds here at the track. The race is set for tomorrow afternoon. With any luck the local bookies won't hear a peep about most of the out-of-town bets—maybe not any of them. Tenstrike will begin the race at two-to-one odds instead of the three-to-two he might have fallen to if the bet had been placed with a Saratoga bookmaker. On a hundred-thousand-dollar bet, that's a payoff difference of fifty thousand dollars."

Winklemann nodded. "Very good—assuming your arithmetic's right and the bet's going down on the match race."

"But the bet has to be on Tenstrike," I went on. "Another hundred thousand on The Mogul wouldn't change the odds enough to make all the hanky-panky worthwhile. And to pay off, Tenstrike would have to win, naturally."

"Naturally," said Winklemann. He found the pencil with the broken point and began tapping it on his desk again. When he spoke his voice was perfectly flat. "I don't think you killed Gibbons, or Sharples or Robinette either. I think you're just the kind of plain damn fool who wanders in front of trains. But listen to me very carefully, Moretti. Don't make up theories, and don't try to be a detective."

I smiled ingratiatingly and started to answer, but he cut me off. "Shut up. I can see your mind working. You can hardly wait to get out of here and begin asking people questions, and maybe leaking a little information to get them started. Well, you're not going to do it. If I find out you've said anything to anybody about what we've talked about in this office, I'll put you in a cell and hold you as a material witness until after the race tomorrow. You'll remember your stay for a long, long time."

"You have my solemn word, Captain. Let detectives be detectives and reporters be reporters, is what I say!"

"And another thing. I want to see any story you write before it goes out over the wire."

"Oh, now wait a minute, Captain! I can't do that! Think of Peter Zenger—think of the Bill of Rights! Surely now you can't be expecting a self-respecting member of the Fourth Estate to betray his birthright and submit to censorship! Why, if I was to agree to that, I'd never be able to hold my head up—"

"You show me any story you write," he repeated. "I'm not going to argue with you, Moretti."

I abandoned the brogue and spoke quietly and earnestly. "You can't expect a reporter to accept conditions like that, Captain. You don't even have the right to ask. This isn't wartime—there's no state of martial law declared here. What's more, it's discrimination—I'm damn sure you're not asking the boys from the big New York dailies to clear their stories with you. The only reason you think you can do it to me is because I work for a national weekly!"

"No, that's not true," he said gruffly. "The reason I'm going to do it to you is because you're the only reporter here who has any chance of digging up some of the facts before I'm ready to give them out." He popped his large knuckles moodily. "I said you're the kind of plain damn fool who wanders in front of trains. Well, that seems to be the way you work on a story; you get drunk and let murderers hit you on the head. If you don't mind the wear and tear on the head, I guess it gets you close to a lot of murderers.

"You want to get your stories that way, it's fine with me," he continued. "But when it's my town you're writing about, I don't want to read about it for the first time along with two thousand other horse-players in *The Spirit of the Times*. I want to read it in advance, right here at my desk, where I have a chance of fixing things before it's too late."

"Every police chief in the country would like to censor the news if he could, but you're the only one I've ever known try to do it!" I said.

"I don't know about every police chief in the country. I only know about me here in Saratoga." He hesitated, and then began to speak in a different voice. "Let me tell you about this town, Moretti. There's no other place like it in the U.S., maybe not in the whole world. It's a little hick town with some funny-tasting water that may or may not be good for you. It's owned by a few farmers who trace their holdings back to before the French and Indian War, and don't like much that's happened since. During the winter you could fire a Gatling gun down Broadway at high noon and not hit anything but frostbitten sparrows. There's not what you'd call a real big demand for policemen, naturally.

"Then, come summer, the richest people in the world start to arrive. Vanderbilt, Jay Gould, Lennie Jerome, James J. Hill. Diamond Jim Brady with Lillian Russell in tow. Victor Herbert leading his orchestra in the garden and John Philip Sousa leading his band in the park. Politicians, bankers, actors, writers, European nobility, playboys—you name it, if they got money, they're here. And all summer long, that money burns a hole in their pockets. The smartest gamblers in the country are running the casinos, and they can't take the money away fast enough to suit these people. Bet-a-Million Gates will bet you five thousand dollars on which fly will land on a sugar cube first, for God's sake! The smell of that money is pulling in every crook in a thousand-mile radius, and who's supposed to keep the customers from being picked cleaner than a boardinghouse turkey at Thanksgiving?"

"The faithful wintertime-sized Police Department?" I hazarded.

"That's right—the faithful seven-man wintertime-sized Police Department!" Winklemann snorted. "I'll tell you the truth, Moretti—all summer long we're sitting on the edge of a volcano, and it gets the worst in August, when racing season starts, and the bookies and the touts show up. The only way in the world I can keep on top of it is with advance information."

"Why don't you hire more policemen in the summer?"

"The attitude upstairs is that we have enough for ourselves, and if the foreigners need more in the summer, let *them* worry about it. Of course the attitude upstairs is also that it would be a shame if the hotels and casinos weren't full all summer long, because that would cost *us* money."

"I can see your problem. But I can't agree it gives you the right to look over my stories before I file them."

Winklemann looked at me levelly. His square red face wore an expression of tired determination. He looked like a man who was committed to something he didn't particularly believe in, and was unwilling or unable to apologize. "I'm not saying it's a right, I'm just saying I'm going to do it. If you want to operate in Saratoga, bring your stories here before you send them. Otherwise, leave town, Moretti."

Any more discussion was obviously superfluous. I rose to leave. Winklemann turned away and began to inspect a paper on his desk. As I turned the doorknob he called after me, "Remember, Moretti—don't make up theories, and don't try to be a detective." I closed the door without answering.

Outside there were three reporters waiting to interview *me*. I didn't tell them anything, but it was an exciting experience.

8

Experiences to Open the Inner Eye

I went out to the track and spent four hours acting like a reporter for a sporting weekly. In general the horses did what was expected of them. Ike Murphy had mounts in three races, and won on two, riding the same way he usually did: not pushing the horses more than necessary and winning by only one or two lengths even when he could have lengthened his lead with the whip. Jackie McCandless also had three mounts, but in different races from those in which Ike rode. He won one, placed in one and ran out of the money in the third. It seemed to me that he might have pulled his horse in his third race, but no one raised a question about it, so I was probably wrong.

Between races I talked to owners and trainers while avoiding conversations with other newspapermen. I received a number of tips on upcoming races, but bet on none of them. Later I figured that if I had bet one dollar each on the first seven and one thousand dollars on the eighth, I would have ended the day $19,993.00 to the good. *C'est la vie.*

I kept an eye peeled for the brothers Dunne, and late in

the afternoon my vigilance was rewarded. I found them by the paddock inspecting the horses on parade. I approached them politely. "Good afternoon, gentlemen. I wonder if you'd be good enough to give me a few moments of your time if it's convenient."

Tom Dunne, the younger brother, turned to me angrily, but before he could open his sullen mouth the older Fergus interposed. "Ahh, it's our friend from *The Spirit of the Times,* Thomas, come no doubt to solicit our views on the day's racing. Good afternoon, Mr. Moretti—my brother and I were quite interested in your last story." The pale liver-spotted skin of his face hung as slackly as a sail on a becalmed ship, but his eyes were quick. His thin purple lips pulled back from his obviously false teeth in a parody of a smile.

I waved my hand deprecatingly. "I hope you won't hold me accountable for that—I have an editor with an over-zealous imagination. I could write a description of a flower show and he'd make it sound like the last days of Chinese Gordon at Khartoum."

"Nevertheless, you certainly seem to have kept busy. My brother and I will be looking forward to your next column eagerly, won't we, Thomas?" The most agreeable sound Tom could come up with was a grunt. "Well, Mr. Moretti, you've found us, and we are at your disposal," Fergus went on genially. "What do you wish to ask us?"

I asked about Tenstrike's chances against The Mogul the next day, and Dunne predicted an upset victory. "He's absolutely in the pink, and Jackie says he's never run better. We have no doubt about the result."

"Are you betting on him, Mr. Dunne?"

"I'm not a gambling man, Mr. Moretti, but then again I don't consider this a gamble. Certainly I'm betting on him."

"Do you like the odds?"

Dunne's smile broadened until the ends disappeared in the slack skin on either side. "Sometimes it's desirable to hold minority opinions, particularly if you turn out to be correct. I only wish we were more in the minority this time."

"Are your friends betting on Tenstrike too, Mr. Dunne?"

He frowned slightly. "Which friends do you have in mind, sir?"

"I was thinking of Face Hogan for one," I said recklessly.

Tom made a movement toward me. His brother touched him on the arm and he immediately froze. Fergus' frown deepened into an expression of friendly concern. "I don't believe I recognize that name," he said.

"Oh? It was my impression he was an employee of yours."

"Hogan—Hogan," Dunne mused. "What was that first name? Face? Face Hogan?" He turned to his brother interrogatively. "I do seem to remember a party by that name, or something like it, don't you, Thomas? Two or three years ago, wasn't it? Some trifling business back in New York? Or perhaps not. In any case—" he said, turning back to me, "—I certainly wouldn't class him as a friend of ours. I'm afraid your information is in error."

"It surely wouldn't be the first time," I said. "None of us has all the answers. Not even my friend Sharples, although I guess he had more than was good for him. Wouldn't you say so, Mr. Dunne?" I addressed this question to Tom, hoping to surprise a reaction from him.

Fergus was too quick for me. "Sharples—isn't he the poor fellow they found dead beside the road last night? Remember, Thomas, we heard about it at breakfast. One of your colleagues, wasn't he, Mr. Moretti? One of your colleagues in that dangerous trade of yours?"

The parading horses had left the paddock, as had most of the spectators. The Dunnes and I were almost alone beside the fence. From the track came the clear bugle notes signaling the next race. I felt a momentary chill. "Yes, he was a colleague," I said. "He did a column for *The Thoroughbred Record*, signed 'Centaur.' We frequently exchanged information."

"In that case I imagine you'll miss him," Fergus Dunne said solicitously. "Was there anything else you wanted to ask about?"

"What odds have you been getting on Tenstrike, Mr. Dunne?" I tried to make the question sound casual.

"The same as everyone else—I think it's two to one, isn't it, Thomas?" The younger Dunne nodded silently.

"That's with bookmakers here at the track?" I asked. "I mean, you haven't placed any out-of-town bets for any reason, have you?"

Fergus Dunne's eyes narrowed. He stretched his skinny neck and straightened his shoulders. "Mr. Moretti, I'll pay you the compliment of being frank with you. I don't understand your questions, and I don't like them. We're backing our horse, naturally. The amount we're betting, and the bookmaker or bookmakers we're betting it with, are no concern of yours, your editor's or the vast reading public whose curiosity you presumably satisfy."

"Did Sharples happen to ask you the same questions?" I took a step away from them as I spoke, but it was an insufficient precaution. Disregarding his brother's upraised hand, Tom Dunne caught me by the lapels of my jacket, raised my feet six inches from the ground and shook me till my teeth rattled together like dice in a cup. He made a fist of one hand and drew it back, holding me easily in position for the blow with the other hand. I covered my face and closed my eyes.

Fergus Dunne intervened. His voice cracked as he seized

Tom's cocked arm with both hands. "Thomas, stop it! Put him down! Do you hear me? Put him down!" He threw his full weight on his brother's forearm, raising his feet in the air. "Not here, Thomas, not here!"

Whether it was Fergus' words or his weight that made the difference, Tom's massive arm slowly dropped and he lowered me to the ground. I swayed unsteadily, like a land-lubber on a rolling ship. Fergus regained his footing at the same time. I tried to pat the wrinkles out of my lapels as I watched Tom warily. "You could always say you had no comment," I said.

Fergus Dunne regarded me with a half-smile. "I don't believe there would be any advantage in continuing this interview," he said politely. "Our condolences on the loss of a colleague, Mr. Moretti. We hope it's all you lose at Saratoga. Don't we, Thomas?"

Tom looked as if he couldn't decide what to do with his hands, and thrust them into his trousers pockets. "Yeah, but I wouldn't make book on it," he said.

The brothers walked away from me toward the stands. I remained standing by the paddock rail. I heard the roar of the crowd as the next race began. After a few seconds my nervous tension began to leave me, and I slumped against the supports. I became aware of a jumping muscle at the outer corner of my left eye. *Paddy, me lad, you didn't make yourself any friends today,* I thought.

I walked away from the paddock and along the rear of the grandstand. I didn't realize why I was walking that way until I saw the small, colorful figure standing beside a door and smoking a long, fat cigar. It was, of course, Isaac Murphy in his racing silks, stealing a quiet quarter of an hour before his next race.

He greeted me warmly, his fine white teeth contrasting with his copper skin. "Paddy, what's happening in this town?'' he demanded. ''They say that newspaper friend of yours was found murdered today.''

''And not only him,'' I answered. ''You remember the charming Gus Gibbons? They found him in his rooming house this morning with his belly opened up a foot. As a matter of fact, *they* didn't find him—*I* found him. And I have a very weak explanation of what I was doing in his room.''

Ike shook his head slowly. ''Three dead men in a week, and all of them murdered. What's got into people around here? I've never seen a race meeting like this in my life.''

''You still have that pressure feeling you told me about?''

He looked up at me quickly from under lowered brows. ''Seems like it's pushing down more than ever. Sometimes when I'm all alone it feels like there's somebody else in the room with me—or maybe not some*body*, maybe some*thing.*'' He frowned at his inch-long cigar ash. ''I always liked coming to Saratoga, Paddy, but I tell you, I'll be glad to leave this year.''

We talked until it was time for the next race. As Ike ground out his cigar butt under his boot heel he said, ''I'm planning to spend the night in The Mogul's stall tonight. If you want to keep me company a while, come along.''

''I don't think Mr. Howard Fowler would like that too much.''

He shrugged his shoulders. ''To tell you the whole damn truth, Paddy, I'm about at the end of caring what Mr. Howard Fowler would like.''

''Then I just might take you up on it. Shall I bring out a bottle of something?''

''Just mineral water for me.'' He grinned. ''I'll drink it and pretend it's champagne.''

I stayed at the track another two hours and then went back to the hotel to write my description of the day's races.

Mindful of Captain Winklemann's requisite censorship, I adhered strictly to the subject—no references to bodies in dumbwaiters, in rooming houses or under trees, nothing about swindles or scandals or reporters attacked in meat storage rooms. It was a story, I reflected, which would bring small satisfaction to the heart of Otto Hochmuth.

As I was crossing the lobby I detoured past the front desk. There was a note in my box. It was written on pale blue paper that carried the faint aroma of English lavender:

Dear Paddy Moretti,

I'm sorry to say goodbye to you in this impersonal fashion, but Mrs. Murchison and I are leaving by the afternoon train. It seems Captain Winklemann has become aware of our presence in Saratoga Springs. Obviously two such desperate criminals cannot be allowed to remain even overnight, lest they corrupt their pure-spirited neighbors in this spiritual retreat.

Thank you for trying to help us with our financial problem. Somehow we will manage to survive in our straitened circumstances, I have no doubt.

Perhaps it is just as well that I am leaving without seeing you again.

Your friend,
Kate Linnett

I called the desk clerk over. "Did you put this note in my box?" I asked.

He sniffed the paper carefully and nodded with satisfaction. "English lavender. Yes, I believe I did."

"How long ago?"

"Two or three hours ago—during the midafternoon. The young lady—Mrs. Murchison's companion—gave it to me as they were checking out."

"Was Mrs. Murchison with her?"

"Yes, sir, she was in her wheelchair. A lively old lady, just as bright as a button. She told me how much she enjoyed her stay with us." He regarded me with goiterous eyes and smiled in a proprietary manner. "It's just wonderful what a few days of taking the waters will do for some old people."

"Isn't it? Did they go to the station?"

"I imagine so. The New York train leaves at three-fifteen, and they had plenty of time to make it."

I thanked him and left the hotel. Since there was no use going to the railroad station now, I went to see Captain Winklemann. He looked up as I entered his office, noticed the folded sheets of foolscap I was holding and reached out his square hand. "Lemme see it," he said gruffly.

I waited in silence until he had finished skimming the story. He handed it back to me. "All right, send it off. Now that wasn't so hard, was it?"

"How did you know Mrs. Murchison was in town? Do you check all the hotel registers?"

He raised a wooly eyebrow almost imperceptibly. "When I need to. This time I didn't need to. You told me."

"*I* told you?"

"That's right. With that elaborately casual way you mentioned her. 'Oh, just a girl I met at the hotel—just sort of a nurse-companion for a poor sweet old crippled lady.' Who in the world would want to pry into an innocent setup like that? Well, I would, for one."

"I mentioned her name, too," I said bitterly.

"Yes, you did, but I wouldn't have placed her from that. It was your manner that gave you away." He grinned suddenly. "Don't ever play poker with the big boys, Moretti."

"So you warned them out of town? Don't you know that

old woman was sick? How could you order her on a long, uncomfortable train ride? You're probably killing her!''

"I understand she looked healthy enough this morning. Anyway, the point is, she's a crook. She works a bogus séance game that got her kicked out of Newport and black-listed in every other resort in the Northeast. She knows what to expect. So does that assistant of hers, that Kate Linnett whose reputation you're so careful of. That's all cut and dried. The only thing I'm not sure about—'' he leaned forward, eyes narrowed—"is whether or not *you* knew about the séance swindle, Moretti.''

My instinct for self-preservation put an end to further recriminations about Winklemann's heartlessness. "Captain, as a citizen of this nation and a toiler in the vineyard of Truth, is it likely I'd be one to hold information from the duly constituted enforcers of the Law?'' Before he could answer, I went on: "You've made my responsibilities clear to me, even if I hadn't known them before, which I did. That's why your question shocks me so.''

"It does, does it?'' He regarded me with a kind of sad patience, as if he were facing an unhappy aspect of his own life. "All right, Moretti. Go file your story.''

I started out the door. "Thank you, Captain.'' I paused. "Anything new on Face Hogan?''

He shook his head, and I left the office.

At the railroad station I ascertained that the 3:15 train for New York had indeed left on time and Mrs. Murchison and Kate had left on it. Then I dispatched my story, along with an appropriate mental salutation to my editor.

Walking back toward the hotel, my way led me past a side street that seemed familiar. I turned into it, and a few moments later stood before a small bungalow set far back from the street under two great elms.

I knocked on the door and waited. There was no re-sponse. I knocked again, and after a few seconds tried the knob. It turned, and I pushed the door open. "Taffy?" I called. "Taffy? Are you here? It's Paddy Moretti." There was only silence.

I entered the house and closed the door behind me. The air was stuffy, and its stuffiness made it seem dense. It was almost an effort to push through it into the sparsely furnished living room. "Taffy?" I called again. "Are you here?"

He was here. His heavy old body, dressed in a checkered flannel nightshirt, lay sprawled near the door to his bedroom. The bare legs with their fuzz of colorless hair were bent at the knee and spread apart as if he were running, his head was thrown back and his eyes were rolled up so that half the irises were concealed by the upper lids. His mouth was twisted in a grimace of pain.

I knelt down beside the body and touched the skin of his forehead. It was quite cool and firm. I tried to move his hand and found the wrist joint was stiff. There was an empty glass on the floor beside him. I picked it up and sniffed it. I detected a very faint smell of Irish whiskey.

Oh, Taffy, I thought, *did the boredom and loneliness finally make you decide to get drunk one more time, no matter what it cost?* I rose slowly to my feet, gazing at the contorted face below me. *And was it worth it?* It didn't look as if it had been an easy way to go, but then how hard had it been to stay?

There were no wounds or bruises on the body, and no smell I could detect on the lips except whiskey. No reason to suspect foul play, I reflected gratefully. Another encounter with foul play would be disastrous. To report discovering the body of another murder victim would mean an automatic trip to a jail cell for an indefinite period—I had no delusions about that. Winklemann had been exceedingly open-minded for a policeman so far, but there are limits to the tolerance to be expected from even the most unprejudiced bluecoat, and the discovery of two corpses in two days, both done to death by a person or persons unknown, must place the discoverer well beyond those limits.

There was a small desk in one corner of the room. It was tidy with an old man's tidiness; there was nothing on it but a penholder and a package of penpoints of various shapes, a blotter, a dozen sheets of plain white letter paper, and a half-dozen blank envelopes. The blotter was almost new, and bore no readable mirror-image words. A row of pigeonholes along the back contained a few personal letters, mainly from family members, all rather distant in tone. There was also some business correspondence from a New York City bank and an insurance company.

I pulled open the three desk drawers. The first was empty; the second contained a variety of supplies, among them a ruler, rubber bands, scissors, mucilage and a small but powerful engraver's glass; and the third was almost filled by a black enameled steel box. It was unlocked, and I opened it to discover another group of letters.

These letters, however, were not about family or business matters; the signatures alone told me that: The Big-Ass Kid, Bottles Bohaney; Little Shiv Loomis, Horsehead Hannigan, Willie the Pretzel and One-Way Butts were the names formally written or hand-printed at the bottom of the first six letters.

It was Taffy's professional correspondence file, or the nearest thing to it. All of the letters in the box—there were twenty or so—were postmarked within the past three months; if he had retained any older correspondence, I found no evidence of it. It is likelier, I think, that he saved these letters until his black box was filled, and then threw away the oldest ones to make way for new arrivals. With his encyclopedic memory he didn't need them for reference, so he probably kept the most recent purely for entertainment.

And entertaining they were. The Big-Ass Kid and Horsehead Hannigan were apparently confidence men, Bottles Bohaney was a fence for stolen valuables, Willie the Pretzel was a stall in a whiz mob (a group of pickpockets), One-Way Butts was a burglar, and Little Shiv Loomis performed as his nickname would cause one to expect. They were not at all reticent; as I skimmed through the first six letters, I learned details connected with a number of the most daring and ingenious crimes in recent history. But only as anecdotes—these were letters to an interested and knowledgeable friend, not reports to a detective from informers. None would have constituted evidence in court, even if Taffy had ever wished to present it as such, which was something he never would have done. For if Taffy had ever felt he was the automatic enemy of lawbreakers, it was an idea he had given up at his retirement. What remained was the old-soldier camaraderie of men who remembered when they faced each other on opposite sides of Cemetery Ridge.

I flipped through the letters nervously, fascinated by their subject matter and yet impatient to be finished and out of there. On the second page of Horsehead Hannigan's missive a notation in the margin caught my eye. The text beside it read, "Remember Duke Ramirez, the serpent of San Antone? He's come up with a dandy switch on the old Prisoner, complete with royal romance, bloody revolution, a mad scene out of Lucia di Lammermoor, a faithful old retainer and a changeling Prince, all handled with the Spic bravura you'd expect. Too bad he couldn't copyright it—I understand his assistant set up shop for himself and is now working the same dodge. Some people don't know the meaning of the word Honesty." The marginal notation beside this passage read as follows:

                        ?
                       F.R.
              M & C? Match purse?
                Pass on to Paddy

I stared at the letters and formed them with my lips.
"F.R." I whispered. Those initials, at least, presented no
problem. "M & C?" I went on. "Match purse?" Match
purse obviously referred to tomorrow's race between The
Mogul and Tenstrike. The letters M and C referred to—
absolutely nothing I could think of.

"Pass on to Paddy" he had written. That meant he
thought the information contained in, or implied by, Horsehead Hannigan's letter would be of value to me, presumably in helping me handle the problem I had discussed with
him. What exactly had we talked about? I closed my eyes
and tried to remember our conversation. To begin with, the
discovery of the body in the dumbwaiter, the body he had
identified from my description as that of Frog Robinette,
who must certainly be the "F.R." of the notation. He had
gone on to tell me Robinette's history, and had mentioned
Duke Ramirez in the process. He had described the me-
chanics of the Spanish Prisoner swindle. We had discussed
Chief Winklemann and Sharples and Gus Gibbons briefly.
Was there anything else? Not that I could remember.

Then what had Taffy seen in Horsehead Hannigan's letter that he had wanted to pass on to me?

I shook my head in frustration and leafed through the
remaining letters, but found nothing more of interest. I
replaced them in the black metal box and slid it back to its
place in the desk drawer, then surveyed the room helplessly. Taffy the Welshman's body sprawled on the thread-
bare rug, the checkered flannel nightshirt hiked shamelessly

high on the pallid thighs, adding a grotesque touch of indecency to the horror and pity of the scene. I shivered and bent down to pull the hem of the nightshirt over the corpse's knees.

This time Winklemann didn't bother to indulge in threats or recriminations. He listened to my account of finding Taffy's body without interruption. We rode to the elm-shaded bungalow in Saratoga Springs' Black Maria, which departed a few minutes later with the mortal remains of Hugh Llewellyn, and spent a half hour poking through the Welshman's possessions. Winklemann discovered the notation on the margin of Hannigan's letter and quizzed me about it. I told him everything I could remember about my conversation with Taffy. He waited impatiently until I finished, then demanded, "What does M and C stand for?"

"I haven't the faintest idea, Captain. To the best of my recollection those initials were never mentioned between us."

Winklemann grunted and studied the letter again. "Well, it's something connected with your friend Frog Robinette," he said.

I protested that Frog Robinette could be called a friend of mine only in complete disregard of the facts.

"Well, you came up with his name, didn't you?" Winklemann asked dryly.

"Taffy came up with his name!" I pointed out. "I just happened to be in the room with him at the time." My eyes fell on the wrinkled rug where the old man's body had lain. "Captain—he did die of natural causes, didn't he?"

"If you call a bellyful of Irish whiskey natural."

"I mean, there isn't any chance somebody got to him after he'd started drinking, is there?"

He shook his head. "I've seen enough people who died of heart attacks, and he was one of them. I'll ask the sawbones for an opinion, but I think we can take it for granted the whiskey did him in.''

"He was a wonderful old man," I said. "He must have hated living here and being poor."

"It was probably a mistake his coming here to retire," Winklemann said thoughtfully. "This is a great place for summer people who can afford to play the horses and gamble in the casinos, and for other summer people who know how to play the people who play the horses and gamble in the casinos. And for the winter people who own the track and casinos. But for the rest of us—" his mouth twisted suddenly—"it's a lifetime of living like kids with their noses pressed flat against a candy-store window."

"He always loved the races," I said awkwardly. "That's why he came here."

"Well, unless he had money the races didn't love him back. The improvement of the breed isn't a spectator sport. It's a pastime for dues-paying professionals. Unless you can afford to lay some money on the race you're as welcome as the town drunk at a church social."

I wondered how often Winklemann had been made to feel like a loutish hired hand by the Gussie Belmonts and Lennie Jeromes of the Saratoga racing establishment. Something about his expression made my guess it had been more than an occasional thing. I recalled Kate Linnett describing her vigil outside Sherry's restaurant as she watched the glamorous rich arrive. They had been the handsomest men and the most beautiful women she had ever seen, she said. Well, I thought, if you want to be handsome or beautiful, it helps to be rich. And to have an audience to perform before, whether it's made up or working girls in New York City or policemen in Saratoga Springs.

I rose to leave and Winklemann raised no objection. "Any story you write, I want to see it before it goes out," he reminded me.

"The next story I file will be on the match race, Captain. I won't write it until tomorrow afternoon."

"Just be sure I see it before you send it," he repeated. I answered with a polite nod.

When I got back to the hotel I went into the great dining hall. The headwaiter seated me at one of the tables for twenty, in company with nineteen other guests who appeared to belong to the bottom half of the United States Hotel's social iceberg. Those nearest me divided their time between criticizing the food and surreptitiously watching the comings and goings of those fellow diners whose seating at smaller tables indicated membership in a more exalted caste, at least in the mind of the *maître d'*.

At a table for two a few feet away, I recognized the sullen features of Harrison Fowler. He was dining with a woman I took to be his wife. She was tall and thin, with a long, tightly corded neck, surprising red circles of rouge on her hollow cheeks and a bosom as comfortless as a railroad bed. She talked with animation as she ate, her somewhat unfocused eyes moving restlessly about the room and then back to her husband's face at the end of every sentence, as if to reassure herself he was still listening. He didn't bother to answer, but filled his mouth with food at a steady rate, pressing each new mouthful into place as soon as there was room to accommodate it.

The woman on my left, a plump, faded little person whose eyes still retained some of the vivacity of her youth, noticed my interest in the nearby couple. She leaned toward me confidentially. "Those are the Fowlers, the *Harrison* Fowlers," she whispered behind her soft, bejeweled hand. "He owns The Mogul, you know—the famous horse that's going to race tomorrow."

"He looks like he has a lot on his mind," I said.

"Well, I should think he does! Not only the race and

all, but his poor wife too! A lot on his mind is putting it mildly.''

"Now, Wilma," said the man sitting on the other side of her, an undistinguished personage with burnside whiskers and a rabbity nose. "The man doesn't want to hear your gossip."

"What do you mean, 'his poor wife?' " I asked. "What's poor about her?"

"Why, she's so eccentric! She thinks she's surrounded by astral presences."

"You mean she believes in the supernatural?" I asked.

"Why, I should say she does! Not that many of us aren't open-minded about emanations from the Great Beyond—I certainly would never deny the possibility of meaningful contact with Those Who Have Passed Over, no matter what less sensitive people may say—" she paused and shot a sidelong look at her husband, who grunted in reply, then resumed—"but you must admit there's a considerable difference between accepting the possibility of communication across the Gulf, and claiming to exchange daily small talk with deceased royalty."

"Well, I should think there is!" I agreed. "All the difference between healthy curiosity and morbid obsession, surely!" I broke off a piece of bread, buttered it and popped it into my mouth. When I had swallowed it, I asked casually, "You and Mrs. Fowler—have you shared some of the same psychic experiences?"

"Oh, yes! We were both members of the same mystic circle. What an incredible, eye-opening experience—I mean the opening of the Inner Eye, naturally." I nodded my understanding, and her husband muttered his dissent. "We communicated through Oxamilchola, an Aztec warrior, who controlled Mrs. Murchison during the séances."

"Mrs. Murchison? The lady in the wheelchair?"

"What a gifted person! Perhaps being unable to use her

legs has the effect of increasing her other powers, the way being blind can make you more sensitive to music—do you think that's possible?" I said I thought it very likely. She continued: There's just no telling where our circle would have gone if Mrs. Murchison could have stayed with us."

"The looney bin, most likely." her husband grumbled.

"Oh, has Mrs. Murchison left?" I asked innocently.

"Just this afternoon. I understand she and her companion went down to New York on the afternoon train." Her soft, blurred features saddened. "What a shame—just when Oxamilchola had begun to trust us all!"

"You and Mrs. Fowler will both miss the séances a great deal, I suppose," I probed.

"Well, *I* will. But Mrs. Fowler hasn't been meeting with us for some days. Ever since she began to develop her own special relationships through Oxamilchola—with those kings and queens and princes on the Other Side. Mrs. Murchison decided she was a distracting influence on the circle, so she's been meeting with her privately."

"I see." A waiter appeared at my elbow, and I remained silent while he served me my beef burgundy. The vast dining hall hummed with the harmony of appreciative munching and swallowing, accented by ringing silver and tinkling glass, underlined by subdued intestinal rumbles and half-audible belches. I helped myself from the common bowls of corn pudding, broccoli, creamed onions and green beans while another waiter filled my glass with claret.

As I began to eat, the Fowlers finished their meal and left their table, Mr. Fowler rising abruptly and striding toward the door with Mrs. Fowler trotting awkwardly at his heels. My confidante, who was concluding her dinner with French pastry, said through an éclair, "Oh, that poor, eccentric woman. I wouldn't trade with her, even if her husband *does* own The Mogul!"

The burnsided man beside her threw his napkin down on

the table and said, "I, on the other hand, would trade with her husband even if he didn't own a cocker spaniel!"

"Oh, you don't mean that, Blakemore!" his wife said airily, with more confidence than seemed deserved.

The Fowlers disappeared, and I applied myself to my dinner. A few moments later the couple to my left had finished their dessert, and, at the insistence of her husband, my confidante rose from her seat. I rose also. "Your servant, madam," I said with a little bow. She blushed charmingly and sketched a curtsey. "Oh, I was just wondering, ma'am—those kings and queens and princes Mrs. Fowler engaged in small talk: which ones were they?"

"Heavens, *I* don't know!" Her husband took her arm and began to draw her away from the table, but she resisted a moment to say, "They might have been Spanish—some of the words sounded Spanish. Anyway, I'm not sure they have all Passed Over. The king and queen have, I think, but the prince may still be on this side. Somehow, I have that impression—"

"Wilma! I'm sure this gentleman doesn't expect you to discuss the whereabouts of all the spooks you've ever known! Come, please!" Glaring at me like an infuriated rabbit, he gripped his wife's elbow and impelled her before him toward the lobby doors.

I finished my dinner thoughtfully, refusing dessert and taking a glass of port with my coffee. Following the meal I moved to the piazza, where I was lucky enough to find an unoccupied rocking chair. There I lit my cigar and smoked for a half hour, rocking gently and studying the stars through a blue haze of tobacco smoke.

I wonder if the queen has really Passed Over, I said to myself. *Or if perhaps she has left this world without yet moving to the next.*

9

The Prince of Ixtapalapa

It was after eleven o'clock when I arrived at the track stables. The guard at the gate made me wait while he checked with Isaac Murphy in the Mogul's stall, then unbarred the heavy wooden door and swung it open. "I guess it's all right if Ike says it is," he grumbled. I took a step forward. "Wait a minute!" he cried suspiciously. "What's in that bundle there?"

I showed him the bottle I had wrapped in a pillow slip. "It's only mineral water. What some jockeys drink when they have to ride the next day."

He took the bottle, uncorked it and sniffed the contents, and handed it back. "Guess it's all right, then, We gotta check all bottles—no booze allowed in the stables. It's a track rule."

I said I understood. He directed me to The Mogul's stall, on the left about two thirds of the way down. The block-long center aisle was dimly lit by kerosene lanterns hung from nails every thirty or forty feet, and occasional lights in stalls spilled out onto the hard-packed dirt. I passed one lighted stall in which a shirt-sleeved veterinarian and two sweating assistants were working over a horse whose breath wheezed and whistled like steam from a teakettle, and another stall where two grooms had succeeded in ignoring the whinnying of their charge and were playing out a hand of casino on the straw.

The door to The Mogul's stall was closed, and no light shone between or under the boards. I rapped sharply on the wood, and instantly a voice responded, "Who's there?" I identified myself, and a moment later found I was looking into the muzzle of a pistol, an old-fashioned pepperbox with five revolving barrels. "God Almighty, don't shoot!" I cried. "Who would you like me to be?"

"It's Paddy Moretti, all right," said the cool voice of Isaac Murphy. "Put that old pistol away before it blows up, Cokie. Come in and make yourself comfortable, Paddy."

The stall was lit by a single lantern with its wick so low its flame was no larger than a shirt stud. I looked from one to another of its three inhabitants: the wide-eyed black groom in bib overalls, with his antique pistol pointing at his bare feet; the smiling sepia jockey dressed in a velvet lounge jacket, fawn riding breeches and soft, turned-down boots of glove leather; and the great gray stallion glaring nervously down his Roman nose as he scuffed his hoofs on the dirt floor.

I held up my parcel and pulled off the pillow slip. "I brought you your Perrier water, Ike," I said.

Murphy pulled the door closed behind me and then took the bottle. "Why, thank you kindly! I'd forgotten I asked you." He peered at the label in the dim light. "It *is* Perrier. Bless your heart, Paddy. Most people would have brought some of that Saratoga Springs swamp water they serve all over town!"

As far as I can tell all mineral water tastes more like other mineral water than like anything else, even if it is

Perrier and comes from France, but I nodded modestly and said, "I just thought you'd prefer it." Ike took a deep swallow from the bottle, smacked his lips, and professed it to be superior to champagne. He offered some to Cokie the groom and to me, but we both declined, which pleased him.

"Well, sit down and stay a while," he said, waving toward the loose straw piled against the wall. "Old Mogul doesn't mind some more company, so long as you keep your voice down."

I hunkered down in the straw with my back resting against the splintery boards. "Well, watchman, what of the night?"

"Everything's been quiet as can be. We were all asleep when the guard knocked on the door and said you were outside." He stepped over to the horse and put one arm over its neck, patting the firm, smooth flesh. "It's all right, big trouble. Nobody going to bother you. Close your eyes now and go back to sleep." Responding either to his words or the tone of his voice, The Mogul obediently lowered his head as Murphy continued to stroke his neck gently. The groom, Cokie, curled up in the straw and immediately fell asleep, his lips vibrating gently as he snored.

After a minute or two Ike Murphy squatted down beside me and took a deep drink from his bottle of mineral water, then corked it and set it beside him. He cocked his head, listening. The warm, still air was heavy with the night sounds of the stable—slow breathing, the shifting of large bodies, rustling straw and creaking leather, the soggy drumming of urine hitting the hard-packed dirt. Somewhere in the distance a human voice rose in an angry exclamation and was answered by another; the sounds were not repeated. Farther away, a dog barked.

When Murphy spoke again, he spoke in a whisper. "You know something? This time tomorrow I'm going to feel ten years younger. Like a hundred-pound weight's been lifted off my shoulders. I don't care if we win or lose, just so we get it over with before somebody else gets killed.''

"Another person's dead you may not have heard about," I said, matching my voice to his. "Maybe you knew him— Taffy the Welshman? An ex-Pinkerton copper who retired here at the Springs?"

"Taffy the Welshman—yeah, I knew him. Somebody was supposed to have fixed one of the races at Churchill Downs a few years back, and he talked to all us jockeys about it. He seemed like a nice man for a policeman."

"He was."

"How'd he get killed?"

"Looks like he died of a heart attack—that's what Captain Winklemann says. He wasn't supposed to drink anything because of his heart, and apparently he put away a glass or two of Irish right before he died. That would do it."

"I guess it would." Murphy was silent a moment, and when he spoke again, it was to ask a question. "This Taffy the Welshman—he was a friend of yours?"

"He was. It was I who found his body. And yes, before you feel you have to comment on it, Sharples was also a friend of mine—and although I'd hardly call Gus Gibbons a friend, he was certainly an acquaintance. I never set eyes on Frog Robinette before Winklemann showed him to me on a slab at the morgue. But still, three out of four's not bad."

If I had expected Murphy to be abashed by this I was disappointed. "Well, you got to admit it's something to think about, Paddy."

"I know," I bit off a jagged corner of a fingernail and spat it out. "I expect Winklemann's thinking about it a lot."

"Well, you can't hardly blame him. Every time he gets

a new dead body to investigate, there you are right along-side it. A man would have to have a trusting nature indeed not to think it was a mite peculiar."

"I suppose. Ike, are you expecting somebody to try to get at The Mogul tonight?"

"Why no, I'm not expecting it. But I wouldn't say it was impossible, either. It doesn't seem like a good time to take any chances."

"What if I was to tell you there's a hundred and twenty thousand dollars' worth of new money going down on Tenstrike—not here, but with bookies in every big city from Boston to Los Angeles? And all of it going down less than forty-eight hours before racetime?

Murphy hunched his shoulders unconsciously, like a street fighter moving toward an expected altercation. "Then I think there's even more reason to keep old Mogul company tonight. Where'd you hear about the money, Paddy?"

I told him about the list of initial letters and numbers I had found in Gus Gibbons' billfold, and of Winklemann's analysis of their meaning. "The numbers added up to a hundred and twenty," I continued. "The same number as—" I stopped abruptly in midsentence.

"As what?" Murphy glanced sharply at me.

"As—as another number I heard about," I finished lamely. Murphy continued to study me. The Mogul and Cokie breathed heavily in the silence. After a long moment I said, "All right. There's more that I haven't told the police about yet."

"I thought there was. You want to tell me?"

"Maybe I better. There's a girl, her name is Kate Linnett. She works as a kind of nurse-companion for an old woman named Mrs. Murchison. She told me that a few days ago somebody stole a hundred and twenty thousand dollars' worth of negotiable bearer bonds from Mrs. Murchison's room at the United States Hotel.''

Murphy studied me curiously. "I should think Captain Winklemann would be glad to know that," he said.

"I guess he would. Yes, indeed."

"But you haven't told him."

"That's true. To begin with I didn't think the money had any connection with the killings, and when I decided maybe it did, I didn't know how to tell Winklemann without making him wonder why I hadn't told him before."

"You mean he would know you held out on him to protect this Kate Linnett?" asked Murphy dryly.

"He might possible have arrived at that point of view. You've put your finger right on the heart of the problem." I squirmed uncomfortably. "The money forms a connection between Mrs. Murchison and Kate and Gus Gibbons, assuming Gibbons was using Mrs. M.'s stolen money to place his bets on Tenstrike. Frog Robinette and Sharples are connected because Robinette was a con man who specialized in the Spanish Prisoner, and Sharples dropped all sorts of hints to me about the Spanish Prisoner before he died. Sharples also probably knew something about Mrs. Murchison . . .''

"Wait a minute, Paddy," Ike Murphy interrupted. "You're going about twice too fast for me. Who is this Spanish Prisoner?"

"It's a what, not a who." I explained the operation of the confidence game as Taffy the Welshman had explained it to me. "Robinette was an expert in it. It's the way he earned his living, so it's probably what he was doing here in Saratoga. Anyway, what I was going to say was that Sharples probably knew something about Mrs. Murchison, because he made a pun on the word 'medium' in Dirty Helen's the first night I got here . . .'' Ike interrupted again to ask what "medium" had to do with anything, and I explained about Mrs. Murchison's séances. "It was her séances that got her blacklisted," I said. "That's why Mrs. M. and Kate couldn't report the robbery to the police—they were afraid that if they did, Winklemann would simply run them out of town, and they'd never have any chance of getting their money back."

"So Kate got you to start asking questions instead," Murphy prompted.

I nodded glumly. "And for all I know, it was those questions that got Gibbons and Sharples killed. I was so drunk that night I don't know what the hell I said or who I said it to."

Ike Murphy uncorked his bottle of Perrier and raised it to his lips for a deep drink. He belched gently as he replaced the stopper. "Paddy, if I was you, I'd go see this Kate gal and tell her you're going to go see Winklemann tomorrow and put all your cards on the table. And then tomorrow that's just what I'd do. Because if you don't get your nose clean mighty fast, that man is going to fix it so you're blacklisted worse than your lady friends are. You won't be able to get into any racetrack in the United States."

"I can't go see her. She and Mrs. M. left town this afternoon."

Ike whistled softly. "Well, you do seem to have yourself in a box, for a fact."

He folded his hands behind his head and stared at the opposite wall. In the silence I heard The Mogul grunt as he shifted his weight, and Cokie the groom stirred in his sleep, his face as innocent in the dimness as a black cherub's. Somewhere beyond the door I thought I could hear faint whispering and the sound of metal scraping on wood. "Do you hear somebody outside the door?" I asked. Murphy cocked his head and listened, and then the loudest sound I could hear was the beating of my own heart.

He shook his head. "Seems quiet enough to me. But keep on listening good. If anybody comes messing around this stall, I want to have plenty of warning."

As the long night crept past we talked about the match race and the murders. I told him about my last conversation with the Dunne brothers and my question about Face Hogan and the reaction it caused. "He was definitely somebody they didn't want to talk about, Ike. If Winklemann finds him, he may tie the Dunnes to the killings. I'll swear he was in the meat storage room with me, for a starter."

"The Dunnes would have the most to gain if Tenstrike was to win tomorrow," Ike said thoughtfully. "Only, how they going to be sure he'll win? If they planned on doping The Mogul they'd have to be sure of getting to him tonight or tomorrow morning before the race, and how can they be sure of that? They're not getting into this stall tonight, not with me here. Tomorrow he's going to have people around him every minute till racetime—nobody's going to get within twenty feet of him unless they got good business there."

"Could somebody shoot him with a dart—you know, from a blowgun or something?" I asked, feeling foolish.

He was kind enough not to laugh. "Paddy, whatever they do, it's got to be something nobody knows about, otherwise the race will be called off and nobody will win a penny. Somehow I can't see The Mogul getting hit with a dart and standing there quietly keeping it to himself." He shook his head. "No, if the Dunnes are going to put down a hundred and twenty thousand on a horserace, they got to be doggone sure their horse is going to win. And I just don't see how they can be that sure."

Again I thought I heard the sound of surreptitious movement outside our stall. "Listen!" I whispered.

"They wouldn't try to break in—I told you, if they try anything it's got to be something nobody finds out about," the dapper jockey replied, with a more concerned expression than his words indicated. "Anyway, there's plenty of people all around us here in this stable. We just got to start yelling, and we'll have fifty people here before you can say Boo."

"Boo," I said. "Why don't you get your friend Cokie's pistol, just in case?"

Murphy patted the pepperbox where it lay on the straw beside him. "I already have," he said. "Now just you sit back and relax, Paddy, and let's try to figure this thing out."

I heard no more suspicious sounds from outside the stall. Neither did I hear any illuminating comments within the stall. Ike and I passed the night trying to arrange three murders, a confidence game, a séance, a match race and some missing bearer bonds into a comprehensible pattern— and failing completely. Toward morning fatigue crept over me, and I put my head back on the straw and closed my eyes. "Wake me up if you get any sudden answers," I said.

Ike stretched his compact, muscular body and closed his eyes with a sigh. "Good night, Paddy," he said drowsily. Within half a minute he was asleep.

When I awoke it was daytime, and the stable was noisy with the day's routine. Isaac Murphy was on his feet picking straw off his burgundy velvet jacket and fawn breeches, and Cokie was yawning vigorously and scratching himself. I looked at The Mogul and found him regarding me with a friendly but reserved expression. He shifted his weight and nickered softly. "Well, I see we all made it through the night in one piece," I said, struggling to a sitting position.

Murphy extracted a straw from his collar. "Yes, sir. It's the big day, all right." He crossed the stall and gently rubbed the horse's muzzle. "Hey, you big ugly hunk of misfortune and misery, how you feeling this morning? You going to run your legs off for old Uncle Ike?''

The Mogul tossed his head and snorted, then pressed his nose against Murphy's hand again. Cokie said, "The way that horse been running, he going to win by a quarter mile. If he don't, it's 'cause he don't want to, that's all.''

"That's what I think too," Murphy said. "And he's going to want to. Ain't you, Mogul?'' The big gray horse snorted politely and began to eye his feedbag. Murphy laughed and slapped him on the neck. "Cokie, get this old boneyard some oats now, hear?'' He turned to me. "They'll be setting up breakfast directly, Paddy. Let's get something to eat too.''

Cokie left the stall with the nosebag. I said, "I want to try my luck with your boss once more before the race. You think he'll be out here for breakfast this morning?''

Murphy shook his head. "Not on race day. On race day he never shows up till afternoon—says he doesn't want to make everybody more nervous than they are already.''

"That's smart.''

"Well, everybody does something smart once in a while.''

I reflected. "Well, I've got to eat somewhere. I can go into the Springs and see Fowler afterward. Let's go.''

We waited until Cokie got back with the oat-filled nosebag and then left the stall. The stable was full of movement; grooms and exercise boys trotted about their duties, veterinarians and trainers conferred and disagreed, newspaper reporters buttonholed impatient owners, and hangers-on peered into open stalls. Outside, the trestle tables were set up for breakfast, and the smells of cooking meat and coffee hung in the clear air like a benediction. I realized I was hungry.

I breakfasted on lamb kidneys and scrambled eggs, and did myself very well. Ike Murphy contented himself with

toast and coffee. I asked him how he could resist the variety of viands displayed in chafing dishes on the tables,
and he said with a smile, "No point in swallowing it down
if it's just going to come up again. On riding days my
stomach's as skittish as a foal in a thunderstorm."

"Don't you eat anything all day?" I asked through a
mouthful of sherried kidney.

"Not till after the last race. About then I'm ready to tear
off the front leg of the horse I'm riding. The way it works
out, if I won I eat big to celebrate, and if I lost, I eat big
to forget about it." He shook his head ruefully. "Of course
eating big during racing season means having about three
bites of something. Barely enough to keep a bird alive."

"I'm glad I don't have your weight problem. If I don't
eat and drink excessively I fade away." I demonstrated my
need by cramming my mouth full of buttered muffin, and
Murphy gave me a reproachful look.

The sun was well up in the sky when I got back to the
United States Hotel. Breakfast was being served in the dining hall, and the massed eaters rumbled like a waterfall. I
asked the desk clerk the number of Harrison Fowler's room.
He assumed an expression as close to condescension as his
bug-eyes would allow. "Mr. and Mrs. Fowler do not occupy a *room*," he deigned to inform me. "They occupy a
suite."

"All right, what's their suite number?"

He hesitated a moment while he debated whether or not
a person in my social position could be trusted with the
information. Grudgingly he said, "Suite A-twenty-seven."

"A-twenty-seven? What floor is that on?"

"It's not on any *floor*. It's a *cottage* suite, of course."
He rolled his eyes toward the ceiling.

"Try to find it in your heart to forgive me." I left the
lobby and walked along the piazza to the enclosed park,
where the cottage suites were. The front door of A-27 was

half hidden by two remarkable specimens of the topiary art—bushes whose protrusions and concavities seemed to suggest the male and female principles respectively, although so subtly that anyone voicing the thought would be considered the possessor of an evil mind.

How very Saratogan, I thought as I rapped on the door.

It was opened by a maid in a white cap. She had a feather duster in one hand, and a smudge on her small pug nose indicated interrupted housecleaning duties. *"Oui, monsieur?"* she asked briskly.

"I'm Moretti of *The Spirit of the Times,* and I'd like to see Mr. Fowler."

She shrugged her shoulders and made large apologetic eyes. "Meestair Fowler, 'e is not 'ere, monsieur. *Je regrette—*"

"All right, Claudette, I'll take care of this gentleman." The woman I had seen with Fowler in the United States Hotel dining hall appeared behind the maid's back. Claudette retreated into the apartment. Her mistress inspected me with eyes that appeared to be slightly nearsighted. "As she says, my husband is not in at present," she said in a flat rapid voice. "Perhaps there is something I can do for you. I am Mrs. Fowler."

"Thank you, ma'am. I had hoped to ask him a few questions about the match race. Do you know if he'll be back before he goes out to the track?"

She shook her head impatiently. The two spots of rouge on her cheeks gave her a feverish look, and the heavy silver necklace that circled her creped neck made a clinking noise. "No, I don't know anything about his plans. I really have very little interest in them. I don't pay too much attention to horse races."

She looked as if she were about to close the door on me, so I said, "I can see how you would find Oxamilchola more interesting, Mrs. Fowler."

Instantly her expression changed. Her eyes widened in surprise, her body stiffened and she brought her hands together with a sharp clap. "Oh, do you have word? Is there news? Has a message come?" she cried.

"Not exactly. I mean I don't know. Mrs. Murchison had to—Mrs. Murchison left Saratoga yesterday afternoon. I don't know if you knew."

"Oh, no, I didn't!" Her jaw dropped in distress. "Left Saratoga? Why would she do that? Just when everything was moving along so well?" She stared at me blankly for a moment; then, remembering her social duties, she took my arm and drew me into the cottage. "Oh, but come in and sit down, Mr.—Mr. Moretti. We don't have to conduct our conversation in the hall, certainly!"

We went into the sitting room and she ordered tea from the maid as if impatient of the necessary civilities. She seated me on a love seat and perched beside me on not more than two inches of cushion. "Now what do you mean, Mrs. Murchison has left Saratoga?" she demanded. "It's impossible. Not when we were so close!"

"So close to what, Mrs. Fowler?"

She crushed one thin, blue-veined hand in the other. "Why, His Royal Highness, of course. It was only a matter of days, possibly of hours. The plans were all made, the guards had been bribed, the transportation out of the prison was arranged—Oxamilchola said everything was ready."

"Oxamilchola said?"

She brushed away the interruption. "Not as himself, as the Grandee. Oxamilchola was simply Forming The Bridge. It is the Grandee who is on the scene, preparing the Royal Release."

"The—ah, Royal Release," I repeated. "In other words, the release of—" I left the sentence dangling, hoping she would finish it.

She peered at me in sudden suspicion. "Who are you, Mr. Moretti, and what is your connection with this affair?" she demanded.

I assumed a modest expression. "I'm just what I told your maid—a newspaper reporter. I had the pleasure of meeting Mrs. Murchison before she left yesterday, and from the little bit she told me about this remarkable enterprise in which you are engaged I could see it promises to become one of the great newspaper stories of all time." I drew a breath and plunged on: "I think the world may be ready to believe the truth about the Other Side, Mrs. Fowler, and it's my fervent hope that this remarkable adventure will be the means of publicizing that truth." I pulled my notebook and pencil from my pocket. "You may trust me not to jeopardize the Royal Release by publishing prematurely—among my colleagues I am known as The Sphinx."

The maid came in with the tea things, and Mrs. Fowler poured us each a cup. "Milk or lemon, Mr. Moretti?" she asked. I told her milk, and two lumps of sugar. As she doctored up my cup I exchanged glances with Claudette, who rolled her eyes up and let her pretty mouth fall open in an expression of idiocy. I raised my eyebrows and my shoulders slightly.

"That will be all, Claudette," said Mrs. Fowler as she handed me my teacup. "Mr. Moretti and I do not wish to be disturbed."

"Oui, madame." Claudette left the room pausing on the threshold to catch my eye and make a comical face illustrating utter helplessness. Mrs. Fowler took a sip of her tea and set the cup down with a firm clink.

"I do not know how much you know about the Emperor and Empress of Mexico, Mr. Moretti. Most people in America today know very little, I fear."

"Maximilian and Carlota? I know that Louis Napoleon sent them over here during the war to turn Mexico into a

Hapsburg monarchy, but the Mexicans rebelled and the French troops went home, and Juárez captured Maximilian and had him shot. The last I remember reading, Carlota was in a lunatic asylum in France.''

She sniffed. ''And you haven't heard of the Prince of Ixtapalapa?'' I shook my head. ''Of course you haven't. His very existence is one of the most closely guarded secrets in the world. For eighteen years he has lived as a prisoner, cut off from all noble or even gentle society, forgotten or denied by those who might have been expected to risk their lives in his behalf.''

''The Prince . . . of . . . Ixtapalapa?'' I repeated carefully.

''The legitimate son of Maximilian and Carlota, heir to the throne of Mexico,'' Mrs. Fowler explained. ''His Christian name is Francis Joseph, the same as his uncle's—the Emperor of Austria, you know.'' I nodded. ''Did Mrs. Murchison tell you anything about him?'' I said truthfully that Mr. Murchison had told me very little. ''Very well then, I shall tell you the whole story. Take notes, and get it right.''

''Yes, ma'am.''

''Toward the end of eighteen sixty-five the Empress Carlota found herself—ah, *enceinte*. Under any civilized circumstances this would have been an occasion for national rejoicing, since the royal couple had awaited an heir since their marriage eight years before, and the succession was now assured. But, as you know, the circumstances were not civilized. The Indian demagogue Juárez was in revolt against constituted authority, and I am sorry to say that our government was aiding and abetting him in every possible way. The Emperor's subjects were confused, troublemakers were everywhere, and it was thought that an announcement of the Empress's condition might add to the general unrest.'' A long strand of gray hair fell across her forehead and she brushed it back. "In retrospect, no doubt this decision was wrong."

"So there was never a public announcement that the Empress was pregnant?"

"That is correct. As the weeks passed, there never seemed to be a right time for it. The situation worsened. The United States demanded that Louis Napoleon withdraw all the French troops in Mexico, and the wretched little opportunist agreed, leaving the Emperor Maximilian unprotected.

"In the spring of eighteen sixty-six, under the pressure of betrayal and anarchy, Mr. Moretti, the Empress gave birth to a premature child." Mrs. Fowler glared at me as if I were somehow responsible. "After the *accouchement* she was shown the dead body of a baby, and told that her son had not survived the shock of early birth. *It was a lie!* Francis Joseph, the Prince of Ixtapalapa, was alive! Agents of Juárez had cunningly substituted the body of a dead infant in his place, and neither his father nor his poor mother had the slightest inkling of what had transpired!"

I scribbled words in my notebook. "Fantastic!" I said. "What did Juárez' people do with the child?"

She held up a bony hand peremptorily. "Please! Overcome with grief at her terrible loss, the Empress prepared to sail for Europe and plead her husband's cause. As soon as she regained her strength she sailed to France. Louis Napoleon put her off with half-promises and lies, and she got no more satisfaction from the Pope. Faced with hypocrisy and cowardice on all sides, she succumbed to brain fever, and was incarcerated in a mental institution, where she remains to this day.

"Her husband, meanwhile, abandoned by his allies, was captured, court-martialed and executed by the regicide Juárez. And that, so far as the world knows, was the end of the house of Maximilian of Hapsburg."

"But the heir, the Prince of, ah Ixtapalapa—what about him?"

"The Prince was raised by a simple Indian couple, in a village in the mountains of northwestern Mexico. Although he did not know his true identity, his foster parents did, along with a handful of civil servants and politicians."

"Is he alive now, Mrs. Fowler?"

Again she silenced me with a wave of her blue-veined hand. "Now this is the most important thing for you to understand, Mr. Moretti. The Prince is one of those fortunate or unfortunate people born with abilities beyond the comprehension of most of us. He is gifted with remarkable psychic powers, and his talents were recognized at an early age by his foster mother, who is a noted Wise Woman among her own people."

I wrote down 'Mother—wise woman" in my notebook. "What particular psychic powers did, or does, he possess?" I asked.

"He can communicate on the astral plane. It is this gift that makes it possible for him to signal his location to the outside world, no matter how deep and solitary a dungeon imprisons him."

"How did he get into a dungeon, Mrs. Fowler?" I asked.

"It was Porfirio Díaz," she explained, her lips tightening into a bitter line. "When Díaz became president after the death of Juárez, he learned of the Prince's existence from an informer, and immediately ordered his arrest and imprisonment. Francis Joseph has been in solitary confinement for the past five years. Can you imagine?" she exploded. "A prince of royal Hapsburg blood, locked up by mestizos and Indians for *five years*?" Her myopic eyes blazed as if she had been personally attacked.

"I should think Díaz would have had him killed, and gotten it over once and for all," I said.

Mrs. Fowler smiled coldly. "Díaz is too much of a politician for that. He knows that someday it may be to his advantage to produce the heir of Maximilian and Carlota to add legitimacy and respectability to his outlaw government. Meanwhile he pretends ignorance both of the Prince's identity and of his imprisonment. The Prince is not misled, however."

"I gather the Prince knows who he is now?"

"Oh, yes—his foster mother told him the day Díaz' soldiers came to take him away. It was because he knew that he was able to make contact with Oxamilchola."

I felt the way I had when I was a little boy playing blindman's buff, and I was blindfolded, spun around a half-dozen times and released to stumble dizzily in impenetrable darkness. "Make contact with Oxamilchola," I repeated, writing "Oxa—" on my notebook page.

"Oxamilchola," Mrs. Fowler said pedantically, "is Mrs. Murchison's control. He is an Aztec soldier who died during Cortez' conquest, in the year fifteen twenty-one. It is through Oxamilchola that Mrs. Murchison communicates with Those Who Have Passed Over."

"Via the astral plane," I said.

"Via the astral plane," she agreed, nodding.

"But the Prince hasn't passed over," I pointed out.

"Oxamilchola isn't limited to communication between Our Side and The Other. He also Forms The Bridge between two or more persons on Our Side when he chooses."

"Such as Mrs. Murchison and the Prince?"

"And the Grandee of Guadalupe Hidalgo. Without the Grandee, the Royal Release would be impossible. When Oxamilchola discovered the Prince was imprisoned, he suggested the Grandee as the logical person to arrange his release."

I wrote "Grandee Guad-Hid" in my notebook, and looked into Mrs. Fowler's mad eyes. "Tell me, ma'am, did Oxamilchola tell Mrs. Murchison that the Grandee needed money to arrange the Prince's escape?"

"Oh, yes. Last week at our private séance Oxamilchola said the Grandee couldn't raise enough money to handle all the bribery himself. His family has fallen on lean years since the revolution, what with confiscatory taxation and so on, and he simply didn't have the available cash required."

"But fortunately," I said, closing my notebook and slipping it back in my pocket, "you did."

She smiled proudly. "Yes, my bearer bonds—just as negotiable as money, you know. One hundred and twenty thousand dollars' worth of bearer bonds. Wasn't it lucky Harrison hadn't had to take them for business?"

When I left the Fowlers' cottage apartment half an hour later, I bowed over Mrs. Fowler's hand and exchanged glances with Claudette the maid.

"You'll see that the facts are not released prematurely, won't you?" Mrs. Fowler asked, her forehead corrugated with worry. "We mustn't let anything interfere with the Royal Release."

"Trust me." Her fingers in mine were cold. Suddenly I felt touched by her sadness. "The Prince—what type of person is he?" I asked.

Her eyes brightened, and the worry lines disappeared. "Oh, he's a wonderful young man! Brave, resourceful, proud—aware of his heritage without being the slightest bit arrogant about it—and so patient under the circumstances, which would have people twice his age simply frantic with worry!" She lowered her eyes and went on modestly: "Of course, I've never actually heard the Prince himself—Oxamilchola Forms The Bridge between us. But I can tell what he sounds like, just the same. There's a difference that comes into Oxamilchola's voice when the Prince speaks through him—a kind of *clean-cut* quality, a kind of

decency—that tells you all you need to know about him!''
She looked at me proudly, as though she were describing
a child of her own flesh.

Perhaps, I thought, in a way she was.

"Thank you, Mrs. Fowler. Goodbye." I turned and
walked away from the cottage door. A moment later I heard
it close behind me.

I strolled back along the piazza and into the lobby. It
seemed noisier and more crowded than usual. I wondered
why until I remembered again what day it was. Of course:
everyone who ever went out to the track to watch a race
would go today; everyone who ever read a racing sheet or
argued over a horse's handicap would do so today; everyone who ever put a dollar down with a bookmaker would
put two dollars down today. Today was the match race,
the race of the year, and few people in Saratoga Springs
would be talking or thinking about anything else for the
next few hours.

I bought a cigar and walked to the desk. There was a
message in my box. The clerk handed it to me, and I saw
with sudden depression that it was a telegram. I opened it
fatalistically, and read.

PADDY MORETTI, UNITED STATES HOTEL, SARATOGA
SPRINGS, N.Y.

WORLD AWAITS REVELATIONS OF MURDERS SWIN-
DLERS AND ASSORTED SCANDALS STOP ALSO EYEWIT-
NESS ACCOUNT OF MATCH RACE IF CONVENIENT STOP
DONT BE A STRANGER COMMA YOU HEAR QUESTION
MARK

HOCHMUTH

I tore the telegram into tiny pieces and deposited it in a
gleaming brass spittoon already graced with the butt of a

dollar Havana cigar. *Someday, Hochmuth*, I thought grimly, *someday, you Bavarian bratwurst, I'll chop you up and have you with beer. Der Tag, Hochmuth!*

I went up to my room. Before I stretched out on the bed I steadied my nerves with two fingers of bourbon whiskey from my flask. Then I lay down on my back with my fingers laced beneath my head and stared at the ceiling. *The Spanish Prisoner*, I began. *Everything revolves around the Spanish Prisoner. Frog Robinette learned to work it in San Antonio from what's-his-name, Mindarez? Ramirez? Sharples made jokes about "the Prisoner" at Dirty Helen's. Mrs. Murchison's séances and Mrs. Fowler's $120,000 in bearer bonds and Mrs. Murchison's missing $120,000, and the $120,000 in bets that Gus Gibbons was telegraphing to other cities . . .*

The ceiling was discolored, and a crack sketched the outline of a bony-faced woman with a wart on the end of her nose. I closed my eyes.

What did Sharples know? What does Kate Linnett know? What does Winklemann know? At least now I understood the cryptic note written by Taffy the Welshman on the margin of his letter from Horsehead Hannigan. "F.R./M&C? Match Purse?/Pass on the Paddy' *M & C is Maximilian and Carlota. What connects Maximilian and Carlota with the match race purse? One hundred and twenty thousand dollars, of course. One hundred and twenty thousand dollars to be spread out in bets in every big city in the country, so the track odds won't change . . .*

It was somewhere around there that I fell asleep.

10

Match Race

The match race between The Mogul and Tenstrike was the third race of the afternoon, and was due to be run at two or a bit after. I arrived at the track a few minutes before the first race to find all grandstand seats taken and standing room at a premium. I made my way through the boisterous holiday crowd carefully, but even so my toes were trodden upon many times before I reached the betting ring.

A bookmaker I knew called Blossom, due to an unfortunate habitual skin eruption under one ear, was busily taking bets and writing markers. I waited until he was free and then asked him for the odds on the match race.

"Five gets you two on The Mogul. Tenstrike's a straight two-to-one. How are you, Paddy? Who do you like, and how much?"

"You know I can't afford to gamble. Aren't those the same odds you fellows were giving two days ago?"

"That's right. Come on, be a sport for once. How about putting down a double saw? You won't get no better odds from any of these other gazebos." He looked at me with faint hope and prodded his excrescence with his pencil.

I pretended to consider it. "Tenstrike's the money bet," I said thoughtfully. "What do you hear from the sharpshooters? Are any of them waiting till the last minute to get down?"

"Not so far they ain't." He looked puzzled as he put his pencil point into his mouth. He spoke around it. "Tell you the truth, Paddy—if something's going on, I don't know what it is. Straight goods. You can trust me. How about that double saw?"

"Can't do it, Blossom—not as long as I'm the sole support of my widowed mother and four infant sisters back in Ireland." He snorted sadly and turned away to write another marker. I threaded my way through the crowd toward the grandstand. Halfway there a lady nearly impaled me on the point of her parasol. I jackknifed, and when I straightened up again the lady was gone and I was looking at the profile of Face Hogan.

I recognized the brutal features immediately—the flattened nose, tiny eyes, coarse-pored oily skin. I don't know if I actually smelled the bay rum or merely remembered its odor, but the sensation of physical danger was the same, whichever the case. Electric tingles of fear shot through my body, and my heart seemed to expand as if it would break through my ribs and breastbone. I gasped audibly and froze in my tracks.

Hogan was six or seven feet in front of me, and moving to my right. There were a half-dozen other people between us, and the thug was obviously unaware of my proximity; if I had wished, I could have easily ducked down and avoided any confrontation between us. As a matter of fact, that was exactly what I started to do (remember, I began this account by saying I was determined to tell the literal and exact truth!). Then I realized that Hogan had more to lose from a face-to-face encounter than I had: he was wanted by the police and I wasn't, and it was unlikely he could do me physical harm in the middle of a law-abiding, well-policed crowd.

I pushed toward him, elbowing my way between an indignant gentleman with mutton-chop whiskers and a weedy youth with a striped blazer and an almost invisible mustache. "Hogan!" I called. "You there, Face Hogan! I want to talk to you!"

Hogan's face turned toward me and his buttonhole eyes widened in recognition. His mouth fell open and a gold tooth glittered in the sunlight. Instantly he began to push his way away from me through the crowd.

"Hogan, wait a minute!" I cried, thrusting myself between a man and his wife. "I want to ask you some questions, that's all!" But he was moving faster than I was, hurling his bulk forward with a furious force that left angry exclamations in his wake. By the time I reached the spot where I had first seen him, he had disappeared completely.

I found a uniformed policeman nearby and reported the encounter. "It's a man named Face Hogan that Captain Winklemann's looking to question about a murder," I told him. "He's not more than thirty seconds away from where we're standing!"

The policeman looked at me impassively. "There's five thousand people not more than thirty seconds away from where we're standing, and probably a lot of them's murderers or worse," he said. "The problem is finding the bad ones, don't you see. You wouldn't want us to go tearing off through all these people and upsetting them on the day of the big race, now would you?"

I sighed. "At least pass the message on to Winklemann, won't you? Tell him Paddy Moretti just saw Face Hogan near the betting ring."

The policeman promised to pass the word along, and I resumed my way toward the grandstand. A moment later the bugle signaled the day's first race. The crowd around me surged toward the track rail and I moved with them.

I watched the race through my field glasses and made notes on its outcome—it was of no particular interest. As the lucky winners moved to collect their bets and the grumbling losers threw their markers on the ground, I resumed my stroll toward the grandstand, keeping a sharp eye out for Hogan. I didn't see him.

I moved aimlessly through the crowd, occasionally catching sight of a familiar face—an owner, a trainer, a fellow member of the Fourth Estate—and pausing to ask questions, swap tidbits of news and jot down notes. It was a beautiful afternoon, warm but with a gentle breeze, bittersweet with the memory of summer and the certainty of its ending. The sky was almost cloudless. High-flying birds were tiny black v's against the bright aquamarine. Flags stirred quietly on their staffs, and ostrich-feather plumes in hats nodded like ferns in a forest as fashionable ladies discussed upcoming races with their husbands or lovers and gossiped with one another. *Splendid, carefree Saratoga,* I thought as I made my way toward the owners' boxes. *What a shame that avarice and hatred should lurk beneath its shining surface.*

Two men were sitting in Howard Fowler's box, but Fowler wasn't there. I introduced myself to the nearer man, a florid, thick-lipped sportsman dressed in a Donegal tweed shooting-jacket, breeches and boots. His eyes lit up with the anticipation of publicity when I mentioned *The Spirit of the Times.* "Want some knowledgeable background for your story, do you?" he said condescendingly. "Well, I guess we can spare you a minute or two, can't we, Jock?"

His companion, a dyspeptic-looking individual with large gray bags under his bloodshot eyes, shrugged his narrow shoulders. "Spare him a half-hour—I don't give a damn."

He opened a picnic hamper by his feet and considered the bottles which were its exclusive contents.

"I was hoping to find Mr. Fowler here," I said, taking out my notebook and pencil. "Do you expect him soon?"

The florid man dismissed the question with a wave of his hand. "Oh, Fowler's gone down to wet-nurse that damned coon jockey of his. Don't worry about it—I'll tell you anything you need to know about The Mogul." He launched into a statistical monologue listing particulars of The Mogul's recent races. I interrupted as politely as I could:

"Excuse me, Mr.—." I hesitated, and he filled in "Bowker, Colonel Harlan Bowker, of the Pennsylvania Bowkers," in a stern voice. "Excuse me, Colonel Bowker," I resumed, "but in the limited time at my disposal before the match race, I'd prefer to concentrate on the more personal aspects, if you know what I mean." He looked blank, so I went on: "The feelings, the emotions, the dynamic personal relationships that form the warp and woof of the great tapestry called Racing. The statistics I can fill in later—it's the unique behind-the-scenes knowledge of men and motivations that only an insider such as yourself would know that can give my story the special perceptiveness I need."

His eyes widened and he shifted in his seat. "Unique—ah, motivations. Yes indeed." He fingered his waistcoat buttons as his companion extracted a bottle of brandy from the picnic hamper and tugged at the cork with his teeth. "What motivations were you thinking about?" he asked uneasily.

"Mr. Fowler's, to begin with. What emotions he must be feeling now! You said he was wet-nursing his jockey— what did you mean by that, Colonel?"

"Emotions? I don't know. Imagine he's excited—I know I would be, if I were in his boots." He paused reflectively. "Remember a time back in Pennsylvania. Had a filly of mine named Rosalinde matched against Mohawk Girl, and had a damn sight more money riding on her than I could afford. Talk about emotions!'' He gave a barking laugh. ''Hot and cold running chills up the backbone, dark brown taste in the mouth, visions of bankruptcy and ruin and spending the rest of my days behind bars—that the kind of emotions you're talking about? Well, I guess old Harrison's feeling some of the same right now, eh, Jock?''

His companion took his mouth away from the brandy bottle long enough to say, ''Wouldn't be surprised.''

''What did you mean about Mr. Fowler wet-nursing his jockey?'' I asked again.

''Oh, that damn mineral water of his,'' Colonel Bowker said disgustedly. ''The nigger sloshes it down by the bucketful—claims its the only thing he can drink that doesn't put fat on him. If you want to know the truth, I think he can't trust himself with anything stronger, because he's a born drunk. Anyway, nothing would do Harrison but he had to trot down to the jockey room with a bottle of bellywash for him today—that's where he is now.'' He shook his head. ''We Bowkers were strong for the Union—my Uncle Clarence was on John Sedgwick's staff at Chancellorsville, and I've shed my pint of blood for the dear old flag—but I draw the line at treating blacks as if they were white. It's against nature; they don't expect it, in their hearts they don't want it, and they lose all respect for you if you do it. Right, Jock? Jock'll tell you—he's from Maryland. They know their niggers down there.''

Jock had his head in the picnic basket, but he raised it to say, ''You bet your milk-fed ass we do,'' and then returned to contemplation of his bottles.

I said, ''You said Mr. Fowler was probably having visions of bankruptcy and ruin and spending his life behind bars. I assume you mean he may have overextended himself on backing The Mogul?''

Bowker's eyes popped with sudden alarm. ''I said that? I

never did! I never said a single word like that, did I, Jock? Never a single word!" When Jock failed to support his contention, the Colonel rose to his feet and pointed a finger at me. "I know your kind," he cried. "You're a troublemaker, poking around trying to stir up a stink. You watch what you put into that paper of yours, you hear? There are laws in this country to protect people against lying reporters! Now you clear out of here!"

I replaced my notebook and pencil in my pocket. "I'll try not to spell your name wrong, Colonel." I caught Jock's bloodshot eye and bowed curtly. "Thank you for your time, gentlemen."

The bugle signaled the second race as I continued my walk along the box seats. I saw the Dunne brothers surrounded by a boxful of guests, mostly sporting types and worse, men with weasely faces and women who overpainted their deteriorating complexions. Tom Dunne, flushed and noisy, was entertaining the group with a story about the Prince of Wales and the entire chorus line of *Princess Ida;* over his shoulder I caught the eye of his brother Fergus, who immediately turned away. I debated whether to try to force an interview and decided against it; the best I could expect under the circumstances was a refusal to comment, and considering Tom's obviously inebriated condition, a more physical rejection seemed more likely.

I pushed on through the crowd until I heard a woman's voice call, "Hey! Moretti, you shanty-Irish spaghetti-eater, don't you say hello to your friends anymore?" It was Helen Liebowitz, looking out from under a pink ruffled parasol, her raddled face wearing the mischievous grin of a kid playing hookey. Beside her in the box, sitting bolt upright to compensate for his crooked spine, was Mama Sentelli's *alter ego,* Joe Palladaglia.

I joined them in their box and accepted a glass of champagne that was considerably better than I would have gotten in either of their restaurants. I gave a sigh of gratitude. "Don't mention it," Helen said. "Particularly don't mention it around any of my customers. I don't want them getting ideas."

"I promise. What brings you two out to the track? I thought you believed sunlight and fresh air could cause irreversible damage to your health." I helped myself to another glass of champagne.

"To tell you the truth, we think a little of it can go a long way, don't we, Joe?" She smiled possessively at the little hunchback. He nodded his agreement.

"It can rot the brain, *paisan*," he said gravely.

The horses on the track took their places for the second race. I applied myself to binoculars and notebook. The race began; the crowd roared; horses changed their relative positions; a long shot held the lead for a few moments and then lost it again; the two favorites came into the stretch neck and neck, and the favorite-favorite won by half a length. Helen Liebowitz beamed and Joe Palladaglia swore without emotion. "What a boat race. Why did I bet? I must have got too much sun already."

"Ignore him, he's a rotten loser," Helen said delightedly. "Here—sit down." She patted the seat of the chair beside her. "Now tell me: what's the news on the scandal of the century?" Her grin faded as she went on, "That's a hell of a note about your friend Sharples. He couldn't hold his liquor worth a damn, but I liked him. He could be pretty funny if you got to him early enough in the evening. Who did him in, do they know?"

I hesitated, then answered, "Captain Winklemann seems sure it was a professional bully named Face Hogan."

"Face Hogan." Her mouth twisted in a grimace. "The brassknucks boy. Do you know him, Joe?"

Palladaglia carefully removed a loose thread from his lapel. "I know him," he said.

"Brass knuckles were what he used on Sharples," I said. "A very thorough job. I saw the results. I'm not sure his own mother would have known him."

"That bastard Hogan," Helen said, chewing idly on the cuticle of a flame-red fingernail. "He likes that kind of work. Although I never heard of him killing anybody before. Breaking them up and putting them to bed for six months, that's what he makes a living on."

"Everybody gets too enthusiastic once in a while," Joe Palladaglia said. "When you love your work it happens."

"Did he do much work for anybody here at the Springs?" I asked artlessly.

"Didn't Winklemann tell you?" Helen narrowed her eyes. "The word is that he was on the Dunnes' payroll. I don't know if he still is, though. Do you, Joe?" Palladaglia shrugged. "Anyway, that would be my guess," she resumed. "Don't tell anybody I told you. Face hasn't got any reason to be mad at me and I like it that way."

I sipped my champagne and watched the crowd moving restlessly in front of our box. You could tell there was a big race coming; people walked more purposefully, talked louder, even the movements of hands and arms seemed more decisive. Bodies gravitated toward the rail; where they had stood three or four deep for the second race, they were now six and eight deep, and the density was increasing. Women's voices sounded higher pitched, and every man present seemed to be smoking—the bright summer sunlight was tinted a faint smoky blue, like the air in October during leaf-burning time. The tension was contagious, and I was surprised to catch myself in the act of lighting a completely unconsidered cigar.

When the bugle sounded for the third race I was still in the box with Helen Liebowitz and Joe Palladaglia. I considered struggling through the crowd to glimpse the two competing horses in the paddock and then dismissed the idea.

After all, what news-worthy event was likely to transpire during the brief walk around the paddock and out onto the track, under the eyes of thousands of excited bystanders?

It must have been just about this time that Face Hogan tried to slip a ball of paraffin, impregnated with hydrochloric acid, into one of The Mogul's nostrils.

I can't, of course, give an eyewitness account of the episode, but my best reconstruction of it is as follows: Hogan and a confederate (the person I had labeled "Gutrumble" during our encounter in the meat room?) were waiting on opposite sides of the paddock fence for The Mogul and Tenstrike to appear. Somehow they had managed to weaken the fence at the point where the confederate stood. As the two horses began to parade around the oval, a large crowd pressed against the railing to watch. At the moment The Mogul reached the point nearest Hogan, the railing on the confederate's side collapsed with a crash, and the front rank of onlookers found themselves flying into the ring. Their shouts and cries of alarm naturally startled the horses, who shied toward the opposite rail. For a moment Hogan was within a foot or two of The Mogul's head, and all eyes were glued to the human pile-up on the other side of the paddock.

Apparently it was Hogan's plan to insert the ball of acid-soaked paraffin into The Mogul's nostril and anchor it between skin and cartilage in such a way that it would remain in place until it dried out and lost its adhesiveness and was expelled by the horse's breathing. By that time it would have done its work; The Mogul would be drugged and there would be no evidence to show that anything illegal had taken place.

Hogan made a grab for The Mogul's head. Ike Murphy made no reaction but the groom, Cokie, observed the movement and instantly tugged the horse toward the center of the ring. The Mogul responded by balking and rearing;

Cokie's feet left the ground and Murphy's feet left the stir-rups—if the jockey hadn't embraced the horse's neck he would have fallen from the saddle.

Hogan dropped the drugged pellet and turned back into the crowd. Behind him Cokie shouted, "Stop that man—he try to fix The Mogul!" In the uproar very few people heard him. One man made a grab for Hogan's arm, but the thug stiff-armed him and escaped easily into the press of humanity surrounding the paddock, as did his confederate on the other side of the ring.

In a few minutes order was restored. Officials listened to Cokie and found the paraffin pellet. They concluded that an unsuccessful attempt to drug The Mogul had taken place, that it had been thwarted by the groom's vigilance and that there was no reason why the match race should not go on as scheduled. Throughout their deliberations Ike Murphy remained on his mount's back, head lowered and knees raised to his waist by his short stirrups, in the riding pos-ture that Jackie McCandless referred to derisively as "the monkey on the stick." He did not speak to anyone.

The news of the attempted drugging passed quickly through the grandstand. When I heard it I immediately left Helen Liebowitz' box and hurried toward the paddock. Be-fore I could reach it, however, the two horses emerged through the crowd onto the track. Over the heads of the intervening spectators I could see the two jockeys perched on the backs of their mounts; first Jackie McCandless in the purple and yellow silks of the Dunne brothers, tensely alert, head, hands and body in constant motion, and an expression of fierce concentration on his pale, narrow face; then Isaac Murphy in green and buff, shoulders bent and knees high, with so little purchase on the horse's flanks it was hard to see how he stayed on except by balance. He sat in the saddle without moving. His eyes were wide and lips were pressed together in a tight line.

The crowd roared as the horses appeared on the track and moved toward the starting line. I made my way back to Helen's box, where the visibility was better than it would be by the rail. Helen said, "What happened back there?"

"I don't know any more than you do. I met the horses coming out. Whatever it was, I guess it didn't work. They both look pretty chipper to me."

I found I was shouting to make myself heard. Tenstrike, responding to the crowd's excitement and goaded by McCandless' ship, danced and flung his head about like a spoiled debutante crossed in love. By comparison, The Mogul seemed stolid and phlegmatic. He moved slowly into position without waste motion, his big gray body alert but relaxed, his head motionless on his sleek, muscular neck. On his back Ike Murphy was equally undemonstrative.

I heard Joe Palladaglia's voice in my ear. "Look there— I would say that was one very nervous man, wouldn't you?"

Simultaneously Howard Fowler crossed in front of our box. His normally florid face was whey-colored, and there were drops of perspiration on his forehead. He looked straight ahead and hurried along with short steps that seemed mincing because of his pigeon-toed walk. "I wonder," Palladaglia continued thoughtfully, "if maybe that horse of his isn't as chipper as you thought he was."

I leaned over the box rail. "Mr. Fowler!" I called. "Is The Mogul all right, Mr. Fowler? Can you tell us anything about the drugging attempt in the paddock?"

Fowler spun his head toward me and stared through red-rimmed eyes. His mouth opened, but no words emerged. His fingers closed into fists, and he raised one as if to shake it in my face, then let it fall to his side again. He shook his head instead, turned away and hurried up the aisle to his box in the owners' section. I followed him with my eyes, and saw him greeted by Colonel Bowker and his friend Jock.

Helen was also watching him. "He don't exactly look like the most confident man in the world, does he?" she asked in her grating voice. "I'm just as glad I kept my money in my pocketbook for this race."

In a few moments the two horses were in position behind the starting line. A sudden eerie silence fell over the stands as all eyes focused on the starter's flag. I felt a swelling excitement that reminded me of the way I used to feel at the trotting track in Goshen, when horse racing was the moon and stars to me. Both horses seemed nervous now, The Mogul as well as Tenstrike tossing his head impatiently. Jackie McCandless' wiry body communicated tension as he flexed his knees to raise and lower himself in the shortened stirrups, but Isaac Murphy sat stolidly in his saddle, shoulders bent and hands resting on his mount's withers. From the distance it was impossible to make out facial expressions, but I sensed that McCandless' features were twisted with excitement, while Murphy's face was closed and dull.

The moment of tension prolonged and heightened itself—and then the starter's flag dropped, the crowd expelled its collective breath in a single ejaculative gasp and the race was on.

Tenstrike took off as if he had fire under his tail, with McCandless wielding his whip from the first step, slashing down as if to draw blood. The Mogul appeared to hesitate in uncertainty for a split second, and then lurched forward in pursuit. The movement seemed to catch Murphy by surprise; he swayed back until his head and shoulders were above The Mogul's croup, caught himself, threw his weight forward and almost fell onto the horse's neck, where he clung as his mount pounded along the track.

"He's drunk! The sonofabitch is drunk!" cried Helen Liebowitz in my ear. "Look at him! He can't even stay on the god-damned horse!"

As the crowd roared in surprise and outrage, Murphy

struggled into an upright posture, leaning far forward with his face almost touching The Mogul's mane. As if sensing a competent hand on the reins, the big gray stallion stretched his legs and began to run. But he was by now a half-dozen lengths behind Tenstrike.

As The Mogul entered the backstretch, Joe Palladaglia, his binoculars to his eyes, shouted, "Paddy—Jesus, you want to see something? Look at Murphy!"

I tightened the focus of my own glasses on the black jockey. For a moment I couldn't see what Palladaglia meant. Murphy's face was a few inches from The Mogul's neck, his eyes were wide and his mouth was open. He looked as though he were singing or shouting—and then a thin stream of yellow-brown liquid appeared from his lips and stretched out past his green silk-covered shoulder, attenuating and thickening in rhythm to the contractions of his facial muscles.

"He's puking his guts out!" I cried.

"I said he was drunk!" Helen Liebowitz screamed triumphantly.

The two horses were in the middle of the backstretch, The Mogul holding his position six lengths in the rear. McCandless glanced quickly over his shoulder to reassure himself of his lead. Murphy clung to The Mogul's heaving flanks with his knees, his head turned outward and his mouth open in a silent shout, as his vomit spewed behind him like a feathery brown tail.

As Tenstrike entered the far turn The Mogul began to close the gap, seemingly on his own volition, since it was all that Murphy could do to keep his seat, or so it appeared. By the time the gray stallion came out of the turn and entered the stretch he was only a length and a half behind Tenstrike.

Through the glasses I could see that Murphy was no longer vomiting; his head was up and his mouth was clamped tight. The Mogul must have felt the purposeful-

ness of his rider, because he stretched his neck and lengthened his stride, until his nose was almost even with
Tenstrike's rump.

Then McCandless realized his sure win was threatened.
Twisting in his saddle, he raised his whip and brought it
down in a sudden slash that passed directly in front of
Murphy's face on its way to Tenstrike's hip. The crowd's
gasp of surprise was followed by an angry roar.

Murphy's only reaction was to hunch down lower over
The Mogul's neck. The horses were almost head to head
now, pounding down the stretch toward the finish, not more
than eighteen inches apart. "Jesu Maria—do it, you bastard!" and Helen Liebowitz screamed, "Come on, Mogul—oh, sweetheart, come! Come!"—I have no idea what
I shouted, but no doubt it was along the same lines.

Fifty yards from the finish line, The Mogul's nose, nostrils
flaring, pushed ahead of Tenstrike's. Seeing Ike Murphy's set
face moving ahead of him, Jackie McCandless acted in bitter
desperation; with a sudden twist he shortened his right rein
and forced Tenstrike against the Mogul. The smaller horse's
right shoulder struck Murphy's left leg, pinning it between the
two straining animals. His instinctive reaction should have
been to pull his own horse off to the right also, thereby freeing
his leg and also losing precious inches of distance—which was
what McCandless was playing for.

Instead, Ike Murphy drove straight ahead, banking on
The Mogul's speed to free him. The pressure on his leg
must have been both painful and frightening, but he didn't
acknowledge it with as much as a turn of his head. If he
reacted at all, it was to lean even farther forward and lower
his face even closer to The Mogul's neck.

The two horses continued through half the remaining
distance as close as Siamese twins, then suddenly there was
space between them, for The Mogul had drawn half a length
ahead. That was how they crossed the finish line, and the

crowd's roar peaked to an earsplitting crescendo as Ike Murphy straightened to an erect seat and rose in his stirrups as The Mogul slowed to a canter. Behind him a white-faced Jackie McCandless slashed Tenstrike's flank with a vicious and unnecessary whiplash.

"God damn, he did it, didn't he!" Helen cried joyously. "That sweet little coon! I thought he was going to get his leg pinched off!"

I didn't wait to answer, but threw my legs over the railing and pushed myself through the excited crowd toward Harrison Fowler's box. It was slow going, and when I got there Fowler was gone. Colonel Bowker was contentedly adding up betting markers and his friend Jock was inspecting the contents of his picnic hamper. Breathlessly I asked where Fowler had gone.

"Fowler? Damned if I know." Bowker regarded me with great self-satisfaction. "Crackerjack race—made myself two thousand on it. Would have made more, but I had a slight liquidity problem with my assets. What do you suppose was the matter with Murphy at the beginning of the race?" He shrugged off his own question. "Oh well, water under the bridge now. We won, that's the important thing—eh, Jock?"

His companion held a brown bottle up to the light to check its level. "Right," he replied gravely.

"Don't hold with poor sportsmanship, never have," Bowker went on. "No call for McCandless to throw his weight around that way—boy ought to be suspended, and no doubt he will be. But it came out all right in the end, hey?"

Fowler," I repeated. "Where did he go? Down to the winner's circle?"

"How should I know?" He frowned reflectively. "Acted like something was worrying him—didn't seem like a man who's just won the race of the year, not by half. Did he, Jock?" No reply was forthcoming, and he went on: "What was it he said? Something about the end of the line, about this being the end of the line. He wasn't talking about the finish line, either."

"Thank you, Colonel," I said curtly, pushing my way back into the crowded aisle again. Over my shoulder I heard his voice calling, "That's B-O-W-K-E-R, son—of the Pennsylvania Bowkers!"

I didn't bother checking the winner's circle; I was quite sure Fowler wouldn't be there. Instead, I hurried to the carriage turn-around and jumped in the first cab in the line. "United States Hotel," I ordered, "and make believe this horse is The Mogul!"

Mrs. Fowler opened the door of the cottage suite herself. The expression on her bony face was politely expectant. "Oh, Mr. Ahhh—" She let her voice trail off without embarrassment, then resumed: "Won't you come in?" She stepped back and opened the door wide. "Do you have some news from Mrs. Murchison, some word of the Royal Release?"

"Is your husband here, Mrs. Fowler?"

She smiled graciously, as if responding to a mildly irritating interruption. "Why, yes, he came in a minute or two ago."

"Where is he? It's vital that I see him immediately."

She gestured toward the rear of the apartment. "Back in the library. You're welcome to go back—but you may not be able to ask any questions."

I started past her, and was halfway across the sitting room where we had had our last conversation when I heard the muffled sound of a gunshot.

"No, I was afraid you wouldn't," Mrs. Fowler said sympathetically.

I ran to the door beyond which the shot had sounded. It wasn't locked. I turned the knob and entered. Harrison Fowler, his face still petulant in death, sat slumped over a massive walnut desk. His cheek rested in a pool of bright, fresh blood, and more blood was pouring from a large hole under his ear, down along his jawbone and throat. One hand, holding a pistol, rested a few inches from his head. There was a gagging stink of gunpowder in the air.

I checked for a pulse. He had none. I turned to his wife, who had followed me into the room. "He's dead. I'm sorry." She nodded pleasantly, as if I had complimented her taste in furnishings. "What did he say when he came in?" I continued. "Can you remember?"

She frowned slightly. "Something about being ruined—I think he said, 'This is the end of the line,' if I'm not mistaken. And I'm sorry to say he made a very impolite remark about me."

"Anything else you remember?"

"Yes, although I don't know what it means. He said, 'That damned black monkey on a stick' with great vehemence. It was the last thing he said, just as he went into the library. Does that signify anything to you?"

I nodded. "I think it does, Mrs. Fowler." I took her arm and steered her gently back into the sitting room, closing the library door behind me. "Won't you wait in here, ma'am? I'm afraid the police will be here in a few minutes, and they'll be wanting to talk to you."

She seated herself primly on a wine brocade love seat, her skinny knees beneath her skirt pressed together like a schoolgirl's. "You haven't said anything about the Release," she reminded me.

I had started for the front door, but I paused to answer. "I haven't anything to say. As I told you, Mrs. Murchison has left Saratoga. I'm afraid I can't give you any more information than that."

"Perhaps the next time I see her she can place me in contact with Harrison," she said thoughtfully.

I shifted my weight awkwardly. "Perhaps."

"It would be very interesting to hear his impressions of his present surroundings. When we lived here together, we really didn't have too much to talk about, you know."

I agreed that it would be interesting, and went to fetch Captain Winklemann.

It didn't take Winklemann long to uncover enough of Harrison Fowler's financial affairs to indicate the desperate nature of his situation. As he told us in his bleak little office the following afternoon, Fowler was faced with disgrace and a possible jail sentence within a matter of days. "He needed a minimum of three hundred thousand dollars to stay afloat," the square-faced German explained. "What I figure is, he couldn't raise that much by betting on The Mogul, because the odds were too low. But if he could be sure Tenstrike won, and if he could keep his bet from shortening the odds, he could make that three hundred thousand with just a hundred thousand of his own.

"That left him with two big problems, though," Winklemann continued. "How to put the money down without rocking the boat, and how to make sure The Mogul lost the race. The money part we already figured out: he had Gus Gibbons laying bets by telegraph all over the country, and at racetime the odds hadn't changed at all—so that part of it was working all right. At least until Gibbons got killed, it was."

The third person in the office crossed immaculately pressed canary trouser legs. "He figured out how to handle his other problem, too," Ike Murphy said ruefully. "Whatever he put in that mineral water, it cleaned my gut as shiny as a gun barrel. Ugh! I think I was pulling up dirt from under my toenails."

Remembering Helen Liebowitz' comments during the race, I said, "Probably most of the people watching thought you were drunk, Ike. That's what the judges would have said when they ruled you off the track, if you had lost.''

Murphy nodded solemnly. "I know. After the race that bottle of Perrier water Mr. Fowler brought me was gone. No way in the world I could have proved it was drugged— and everybody knows what a hog Ike Murphy is for champagne.''

"When did it hit you, Ike?" I asked.

"When we were in the paddock—it was like I had gotten kicked in the stomach. Then going out through the tunnel onto the track, all of a sudden things started to go round, and I could feel myself getting cold all over. I didn't know what was the matter with me—thought I'd caught double pneumonia or malaria or something. My stomach came up into my throat and I was so weak it was all I could do to hang on the horse. I had to throw up, but I kept telling myself I couldn't, because everybody would see it and think I was drunk. I was working so hard to hold it down I didn't even see the starter's flag.'' He shook his head, marveling. "I tell you, gentlemen, I never spent a worse five minutes in my life, and I never hope to again as long as I live.''

"I was watching you through my glasses," I said. "I saw you when you couldn't hold it any longer. Ah, lad, a spectacular sight it was when you started to spew. The force of the stream pushing backward added wings to your flight. Who knows—without that extra propulsion you might not have won the race!''

"All right, Moretti," Winklemann growled. "Let's get on with it. When you were in the paddock, Mr. Murphy, did you see the man who tried to stick the paraffin ball up The Mogul's nose?''

Ike shook his head. "I wasn't seeing good just then, Captain.''

"Well, we know who it was anyway. It was Face Hogan. Does that name mean anything to you?''

"Only that Paddy mentioned it once."

"What about Hogan?" I asked.

Winklemann's yellow eyebrows rose and fell over his small eyes. "We don't know where he is, but we're looking for him. We'll pick him up if he stays on at the Springs, and we've wired New York City and Albany to keep an eye out for him."

"Was he working for Harrison Fowler, Captain?" I asked.

Winklemann snorted. "Hell no. He was working for the Dunne brothers, same as always. That's the funny part of it. Here were two horses racing, only two, one an odds-on favorite, the other at two-to-one. And the owners of both horses are trying to snaffle the favorite, and neither knows what the other one is doing. Fowler is trying to do it by doping Murphy here, and the Dunnes have got their man Hogan trying to stuff a wad of hydrochloric acid up the horse's nose."

"Then when neither of those methods worked," I said to Murphy, "your friend Jackie McCandless tried to pinch your leg off. You seem to be the only person involved in the race who didn't know what the plan was. Doesn't that make you feel foolish?"

"I don't study 'bout them, I just rides them," the copper-colored jockey said blandly.

I thought a moment. "Face Hogan killed Sharples—the brass knuckles are his trademark. But why? And why did he make a try for me in the meat room at the hotel? Did the Dunnes want us both out of the way because we were sniffing around about the race?"

Winklemann frowned. "We'll find that out when we get Hogan. He may have had something personal against Sharples, or the Dunnes may have told him to scare him off and he overdid it. Either way, he killed Sharples and he'll swing for it."

"All right. And last but not least, who killed Gus Gibbons and our old friend Frog Robinette, if you can remember back that far?"

Captain Winklemann spread his hands as if to caution restraint. "There are some details we'll never know—but it stands to reason Gibbons was killed by Harrison Fowler. He was placing Fowler's telegraph bets for him, so he probably had the money to cover those bets; he was a crook, but he wasn't a fool—he would never have put himself on the hook for a hundred thousand dollars without having the money to pay off in case he lost. Maybe Fowler tried to take his money back, and Gibbons wouldn't give it to him, and Fowler carved up his belly. It could have happened that way."

Isaac Murphy stirred uneasily in his chair. "What you said about me feeling foolish, Paddy—I do and I don't. In a way, I guess I've known for a week that something mighty strange was going on; you remember the first day you came out to the track I told you about the feeling I had about the pressure, how it was stronger in some places than you'd expect, and not as strong as you'd expect in others, how Mr. Fowler and the Dunne brothers and Jackie McCandless all seemed to be getting ready for some other race than the race I was thinking about—I guess something was trying to tell me what was going on, and I was too dumb to understand." He shook his head in bafflement. "But Lord Almighty, how was I supposed to know that *everybody* was trying to throw the race?"

"All right, Captain, that leaves Frog Robinette," I said, in the brisk voice of a reporter anxious to dot the i's and cross the t's. "How do you figure him into all this?"

Captain Winklemann regarded me impassively for a moment. "Well, on the basis of the information I have, I'm not sure I can figure him in at all." He paused, then went on: "It's possible his death didn't have any connection with the match race. He wasn't wearing any clothes, re-member—maybe somebody just found him in the wrong bed, like we figured to begin with.''

"Is that the police theory, Captain?"

His eyes became even smaller and harder than usual, if possible. "That's the only theory the facts we have will support, Moretti. Of course, if we had some other facts we might work up some other theories to go with them.''

Murphy rose from his chair and shook nonexistent wrin-kles out of his canary trouser legs. "Well, Captain, Paddy, this has all been mighty interesting, but like they say, that was yesterday's race, and I got three new ones coming up this afternoon. So, if you gentlemen will excuse me—" he raised a narrow-brimmed derby one shade of brown darker than his skin and set it carefully on his head.

"Wait a minute, Ike, I'll go with you," I said, hurriedly rising and joining him by the door.

"Oh, Moretti, before you go," Winklemann called, "what I told you about any story you file—it still holds. I want to see it before it goes over the wire."

"And don't you have my word, Captain?" I asked in a hurt tone. "For didn't I promise that any story I sent from Saratoga Springs would pass your eye first?"

But Captain Winklemann didn't see my match race story—for two hours later it was folded in my breast pocket and I was boarding the afternoon train for New York City.

11

Champagne with a Beer Chaser

Otto Hochmuth sucked a horehound drop noisily, his mouth puckered into a small, obscene dimple. His round yellowed eyeballs rested loosely in their gray pouches. His sparse and colorless hair was buttered across his liver-spotted pate, his wattled neck drooped folds of skin over his soiled celluloid collar, and his pendulous earlobes trembled like gelatin each time he breathed. Not, I reflected, what you would describe as a physically prepossessing man.

"I look forward to reading this report, Mr. Moretti," he said as he unfolded my story. He glanced over the first paragraph. "I'm pleased to see that you describe the correct horse as the winner. This is in accordance with the traditions of this newspaper. We have found that, although it is sometimes possible to escape censure if we make the same mistake in a field of two." He gazed at me thoughtfully while he swallowed the horehound drop, which caused his Adam's apple to leap above his collar like a startled quail.

With a degree of self-control for which neither the Irish nor the Italian race is noted, I inclined my head. "I'm sure you'll find the facts to be in order, Mr. Hochmuth."

" 'A consummation devoutly to be wished,' as the Bard observes in a somewhat different context," said Hochmuth. "Well, we shall see, shan't we?"

"Meanwhile, if you'll excuse me, I have one or two loose ends to tie up," I said.

Hochmuth waved one hand airily. "By all means re-create the inner man, Mr. Moretti. *Carpe diem,* seize opportunity by the forelock. One never knows how long one will continue to enjoy the opportunity, or be able to afford it."

I walked across the noisy editorial room to the swinging doors that led to the street. I heard the voices of colleagues offering salutations, but responded to none of them. On the sidewalk outside I narrowly avoided colliding with Blinky Malone, the blind street vendor who sold pencils and shoe-laces in front of *The Spirit of the Times* office each day from eight to five. He recoiled, clutching his tray to his bosom. "And who's the ill-mannered scut that tramples a blind man like he was a piece of cow-flop under his feet?" he cried in a sea-gull voice.

"I'm sorry, Blinky. It's me, Paddy Moretti." I found a dime and dropped it into his cup. "I wasn't watching where I was going. I've just been talking to Otto Hochmuth."

"Ah, it's all right, then," the blind man said understandingly. "How have you been, Paddy? You haven't been around for the past few days."

I told him I had been to Saratoga Springs for the match race. He was an avid enthusiast of the Sport of Kings, and wouldn't be satisfied until I had described The Mogul's victory in detail. When I had finished he said, "It would be worth having your eyes back to see a race like that."

"Tell me something, Blinky. If you had two hours to kill before an important meeting, where would you do it?"

He smiled. "Why, where a man can think what he wants, and drink what he wants, and commune with other gentlemen or with his own immortal soul in perfect peace and tranquility. By which I mean McSorley's, of course.''

He was absolutely right. I thanked him for his sage advice and set out on the twenty-minute walk to Cooper Square. The streets were noisy and crowded, full of cursing and laughter and gossip and commerce, and elbow-to-elbow environment that contrasted sharply with the splendid isolation of promenaders in Saratoga Springs. Instead of fiacres, broughams and landaus, the narrow east-west streets were jammed with beer lorries, ice wagons and pushcarts. Smells of food, garbage, sweat and a dozen unclassifiable or indescribable substances were orchestrated like a Mozart symphony. Screaming children dashed between adult legs, scrawny dogs slunk in and out of alleys and impassive cats observed the world from shadowy areaways.

I turned into the musty coolness of McSorley's Old Ale House and bellied up to the bar. Old John McSorley, engaged in an argument with another customer, did not deign to notice my arrival for a minute or two, and I helped myself to a handful of chopped onions and a slice of dessicated cheddar cheese from the free lunch. The onions seemed even stronger than I remembered them, and my eyes were watering when John set a pewter mug of dark ale on the bar before me.

I took my ale and another slice of cheese to a table in the back room. The room was quiet, cool and empty, and so it remained during the hour I spent there. I finished my mug of ale and had three more, thinking long thoughts as I idly studied the portrait of Peter Cooper over the mantelpiece. The voices of the customers in the front room were subdued, hardly more audible than the purring of McSorley's dozen-or-so cats. It was a good time for reflection.

A little after seven o'clock I left McSorley's and caught a hack on Third Avenue. It was dusk, and the city's workaday mood was blending with the anticipatory aura of a late summer evening. I gave my destination to the cabman and settled back against the cracked leather seat.

An hour later, dressed in my hand-me-down dinner clothes, slightly rusty with age but otherwise presentable, I entered the restaurant. The *maitre d'* moved to intercept me as I started across the great glittering room, but I fended him off with a wave of the hand. "Just joining friends," I said.

She was seated at a small table beneath a painting of a shepherd surrounded by three dancing women in diaphanous gowns, heavily framed in gilt. A man was sitting across from her. They were eating oysters and drinking champagne. I stood beside the table and smiled down at her. "Hello, Kate."

For a moment her eyes narrowed and her jaw muscles tightened. Then her face lit up with a delighted smile. "Why, Paddy—Paddy Moretti! How wonderful to see you again—and what a surprise!" She reached out her hand and I took it. The fingers were cool from the chilled champagne glass. "I didn't know Sherry's was one of your hangouts."

I squeezed her fingers briefly and released them. " 'Tis a bit rich for me blood most of the time. But I had a hunch I might find you here." Without waiting for an invitation I pulled over an empty chair from a nearby table and sat down. "You don't mind if I join you, do you?"

Kate opened her mouth to speak, hesitated, glanced quickly at her companion, gave an almost imperceptible shrug and said, "Why, what a treat! Paddy, this is my friend Stanley Beeson. Stanley, Paddy Moretti is the reporter I told you about who was so helpful in Saratoga Springs."

"How do you do?" I said, and put out my hand. Beeson looked at it a moment as if deciding whether or not my acquaintance was worth the gross labor of shaking it. He decided it was, barely. His hand was small and soft, and his grip was as slack as a fishing line after a fish has thrown the hook. He was a small, delicately made man with neat regular features, curly honey-colored hair and a pouting mouth. "How're ya?" he asked, with a touch of Five Points in his languid voice.

I said I was fine. The waiter appeared at my elbow, and I requested a champagne glass. When he brought it I waved him away and filled it myself from the opened bottle in the ice bucket, while Kate and Beeson watched silently. I raised the glass in a solitary toast. "To Mrs. Murchison, may the good Lord bless and keep her. I drink to her with the good wine of Sherry's New York restaurant, the likes of which you won't find in Goshen, Ohio, even if you should ever live there, which is exceedingly unlikely." I drank half the glass and set it down on the white linen cloth. "How is the dear old lady, Kate?"

"Better, I think, wouldn't you say, Stanley? Stanley is a great favorite of Mrs. M.'s, Paddy. Wouldn't you say she was better, Stanley?"

"Yeah, better. Much better." Stanley had, I thought, the voice of a debauched choirboy.

"I'm sure Stanley would know as well as anybody," I said. "Anybody except Frog Robinette, I mean. And unfortunately the Frog can't give us an opinion anymore." I drank the rest of the glass of champagne and refilled it.

Kate's lovely face was expressionless. The fingers of one hand toyed with an antique cameo brooch on a dark silver chain around her neck. "Isn't that the man you mentioned before, the one who was killed in the hotel in Saratoga? Why would he know anything about Mrs. M.?"

I sipped some more champagne. Behind me I heard voices and movement as a new party of diners were seated at an adjacent table. Conversation hummed all around, and there was the comfortable rattle of heavy silver against fine china.

"For the same reason that I'm the world's greatest authority on racing reporters named Moretti. Because he *was* Mrs. Murchison, of course."

Kate Linnett drew a deep breath that molded her full breasts against the moss-green watered satin of her *décolleté* gown. "This Frog Robinette was Mrs. Murchison?" she repeated in an incredulous voice. "Paddy, you're talking the most incredible gibberish!"

The man she had introduced as Stanley Beeson had lost his insouciance. Although he made no movement, I could sense the tensing of muscles in the small, slouching body, and his soft red mouth tightened angrily.

"How much did you give Stanley to come bail you out?" I asked. "Not all of the Frog's share, surely. After all, he only had to appear in costume once, when you were checking out of the hotel. And then ride to the station, and be helped onto the train, and disappear with you into a compartment. That was enough to prove that Mrs. M. was alive and kicking when she left Saratoga." I turned to Beeson. "How much did she give you, Stanley? A hundred dollars? Two hundred? That's a pretty small percentage of a hundred and twenty thousand dollars."

Beeson's eyes flickered toward Kate Linnett. The corners of her mouth drew down. "That's the amount of money Mrs. Murchison lost—I told you that," she said evenly. "But that's the only thing you've said that I can make head or tail of. Mrs. Murchison is taking a nap at our hotel right this minute. If you don't believe me, as apparently you don't, Stanley and I can take you there as soon as we finish dinner."

I shook my head ruefully. "We Morettis may not be among the world's movers and shakers, but my mother never raised any village idiots. No, I think we'll do our talking here amid the happy diners, thank you." I poured myself another glass of champagne, tasted it and thought to myself that it had better be my last one.

"Well, I don't know how much talking I want to do with you, unless you start talking some sense. Really, Paddy!" She laughed and speared an oyster delicately. "I don't know what's come over you. You were so nice back at the Springs!"

I sighed and set my glass down. "All right. I guess you won't believe I know unless I start at the beginning and go right on through to the end. Frog Robinette was a female impersonator—that's why his eyebrows were plucked, and why his face was pitted from white lead face make-up. Taffy the Welshman even told me he played the woman in a badgergame setup in Louisville for a while, but I didn't make the connection."

"The connection?" Kate asked. Her eyes were wide and melting, but a spark of mocking amusement lurked in their depts.

"The connection with a naked male body found in a dumbwaiter. Why was he naked? The obvious conclusion was that he had been that way when he was killed—probably in some bed where he had no business to be. That started the police looking for a missing man, and there *was* no missing man. But what if he hadn't been naked at all when he died? What if he had been fully dressed? In that case he was undressed *after* he died, and his naked body was trundled through the halls of the United States Hotel to the butler's pantry where it was de-elevated to the kitchen below. A complicated procedure, surely. Why would anyone choose to adopt it?

She batted her eyes and said, "I don't know, teacher. Why *would* anyone choose to adopt it?" Across the heavy linen tablecloth from her, Stanley Beeson shifted in his chair and flicked a fingernail against the rim of his water tumbler.

"Because he—or she—couldn't afford to let Robinette's body be discovered in the clothes he was wearing at the time he was killed?" I asked rhetorically. "Lets see—if that were the case, then what kind of inappropriate or unacceptable clothes might Robinette have been wearing?" I paused, then receiving no answer, went on: "What if he were wearing women's clothes, for instance? What if he were involved in a female impersonation, and had no male clothes with him in which his body could be clothed? If his body were to be found dressed in women's clothes the impersonation would be discovered immediately. But if it were found in the nude, there's no reason why the impersonation need be discovered at all."

Kate's mocking eyes and the length of my necessary explanation combined to excite my thirst. I assuaged it by emptying my champagne glass and refilling it against future needs. "The police didn't look for any missing women—why would they? They had an unidentified man's body on their hands. Even when they identified Robinette there was no reason suspect the truth—particularly since no women seemed to be missing. I didn't even suspect—and I had more reason to than anybody else. After all, I had even looked into the old woman's room!"

"Mrs. Murchison? Are you talking about Mrs. Murchison?" Kate asked. "If you are, then you must remember that you saw her asleep in her bed that night." She put her hand lightly on my arm. "Paddy, you worry me. I told you Mrs. M. is asleep back at our hotel right now and see for yourself." She glanced at her companion. "You wouldn't mind too much if we left in the middle of dinner, Stanley? It seems to be so important to Paddy."

I drew my arm away. "Not a chance, Kate. I like it here. I can't usually afford it, but tonight I'm making an exception. I wouldn't miss a minute of my night at Sherry's.''

She drew her full lips together in a moue. "Then I guess you might as well go on with whatever it is you're doing. After you've finished we'll talk about something interesting."

"That business in Mrs. Murchison's room was brilliant. I saw just exactly what you wanted me to see—I looked at a couple of pillows stuffed under the covers in a half-lit bedroom and saw an old woman asleep, because you *showed* her to me." I shook my head admiringly. "It never even crossed my mind that the bed might be empty, not after you took me by the hand and practically led me on a guided tour of her room." I raised my glass in a toast. "Here's to you, Kate. When in an impossible position, attack!" I took a swallow of champagne and set the glass down. For some reason it rocked violently, sloshing liquid on the tablecloth. Kate and Stanley Beeson exchanged a quick glance. Both their faces were slightly blurred. I decided I better get on with it.

"Look, you and Robinette were working a two-level con. On the lower level it was a fake-séance swindle that paid your room and board and brought in the marks. Then you selected one of the marks for the high-level fleecing, which was a very original version of the Spanish Prisoner, played on the astral plane. You convinced Mrs. Harrison Fowler that you could arrange to free the son of Maximilian and Carlota of Mexico, and she brought you a hundred and twenty thousand dollars' worth of bearer bonds to pay for the escape.

"So far, so good. But what you didn't know was that Mrs. Fowler's husband was in serious financial trouble, and was counting on 'borrowing' his wife's bonds to use to bet against his own horse in the match race, because that way he could take advantage of the long odds against Tenstrike. Naturally, he intended to make sure that his own horse lost.

"When Fowler discovered the bonds were gone he must have gone half out of his mind. He realized his wife must have given the bonds to the fake medium she talked so much about, so he hotfooted it to the United States Hotel and came up to Mrs. Murchison's room. You were out somewhere, and Robinette was alone. Whatever happened between them, Robinette made a mistake, and Fowler beat his brains out with his walking stick. Then he found his bonds and took them away with him.

"That must have been quite a moment for you, macushla, when you walked into your partner's room and found his corpse there and the money gone. But if there's any word to describe you, which indeed there may not be, it's resourceful. You realized that if you were to be allowed to stay in Saratoga Springs long enough to find the bonds and get them back, you had to conceal any connection between the fictitious Mrs. Murchison and the deceased Mr. Robinette. So you stripped him mother-naked, waited until the halls were deserted, trundled him to the dumb-waiter in his wheelchair and dispatched him to the nether regions."

" 'Resourceful' certainly seems to be the word, doesn't it, Stanley?" Kate asked dryly, smoothing her auburn hair back from her brow with a graceful hand. Stanley didn't answer, but continued to regard me speculatively.

"The next day," I continued, "you wired for a replacement for Mrs. M., which started Stanley here on his way to Saratoga. Then you set out to recruit an ally in your search for the bearer bonds. The Good Lord in His infinite wisdom decreed that you would choose me." I paused, musing on the inscrutable ways of Providence. "Tell me the truth. Have you ever spent a single day in Goshen, Ohio?"

She lifted the champagne bottle from the ice bucket and filled my glass. For a moment there were two Kates pouring two bottles, but I pulled them back into a single image by an act of will. "Save some for yourself," I said.

"Oh, there's plenty," she answered lightly.

I took a sip. It tasted like cool, fresh autumn air. "I see what you mean about Sherry's, Kate. It's an elegant way of living, surely. A beacon to light a lady's way through life. The pot of gold at the end of the rainbow, guarded by leprechauns in monkey suits serving oysters and bottles of champagne. I'm a believer meself—won't hear a single word against it." I took another sip and regretfully put the glass down.

I went on to tell her how, unbeknownst to both Harrison Fowler and her, the Dunne brothers were also intent on ensuring the victory of Tenstrike in the match race. How their hired bully, Face Hogan, had somehow discovered that my friend Sharples suspected the race would be thrown and that I had questioned Sharples before writing a story for *The Spirit of the Times* hinting at unspecified scandal and fraud. How Hogan and a confederate had attempted to practice their skills on me in the hotel meat storeroom, and how they had later exceeded their intentions by beating poor Sharples to death.

"But none of that had anything to do with the main business at hand, which was the hundred and twenty thousand dollars," I continued. "you put me to hunting it, and when I got too drunk to sort out the information I had, you made me take you back to your hotel room. From there you went on by yourself—right to Gus Gibbons' room. You were guessing that Harrison Fowler was using Gibbons to put that hundred and twenty thousand down with out-of-town bookmakers, so it wouldn't change the track odds—and you were right. You found Gibbons at home. Then I imagine you indulged in a certain amount of conversation and even a touch of lovemaking before you put that six inches of knife-blade into his belly and tried to lift him up on it. Is that true? I hope so. Since the poor spalpeen had to die anyway, I hope he shuffled off with something nice to think about.''

Kate opened her velvet evening purse and put her hand inside. ''Paddy, you're saying outrageous things, and you're going to feel so foolish when you find out how wrong they are. Now I insist that you come back to our hotel and see Mrs. Murchison for yourself.''

I started to shake my head and she allowed the tip of the barrel of a derringer to show above the clasp of her bag. ''Oh, please!'' she said. From the size of the bore, the tiny weapon fired a ball large enough to take off half a man's head.

''Would you use that here in the middle of Sherry's Restaurant?'' I asked unsteadily.

''Do you want to see?'' she countered.

''I don't think so.'' I emptied my champagne glass and stood up. The great dining room swayed and the crystal chandeliers slipped out of focus and became glowing swirls of light. I steadied myself with one hand on the back of my chair. Kate Linnett rose gracefully, and Stanley Beeson also stood up.

''Leave some money, Stanley,'' she said crisply. Beeson produced a billfold, thumbed through bills and laid two twenties on the tablecloth. ''That's forty bucks of mine,'' he said hoarsely. She paid him no attention. ''All right, Paddy, head for the door,'' she told me. ''And try not to fall over anything on the way.''

I raised my hands to the level of my shoulders and began to walk toward the lobby doors. ''Put your hands down!'' Kate hissed in my ear. I hesitated a moment, then slowly lowered them to my sides. ''And be careful—I'm right behind you,'' she added.

It was a long way to walk. I seemed to be looking at my feet through a telescope the wrong way—tiny feet taking tiny steps at the ends of stiltlike legs. When I looked around the dining room I could see people talking and eating, but their voices seemed to come from the end of a tunnel. The faces of waiters swam into view and disappeared like tropical fish in a bowl. My face felt as stiff as a starched shirt-front. I stopped to get better control of my balance, and felt the touch of Kate's evening purse against my back. "Just walk, Paddy," she whispered.

As we approached the lobby doors two other groups of diners were also converging on them. To our left were two men who looked like a tycoon and his secretary, the tycoon dressed in evening clothes and a flowing mustache, the secretary in a shiny blue serge suit and an expression of diffidence; to our right were a self-satisfied man and the cause of his self-satisfaction, a woman obviously too young to be his wife. It appeared that all three groups would reach the double doors simultaneously.

I turned and raised my hands again. "Kate, why don't we have a nightcap and talk this over?" I asked. "I don't know about you, but I for one could do with a snifter of brandy." I smiled as naïvely as I could. "I mean, who knows when we may be at Sherry's again?"

She stared at me in surprised irritation. "Are you crazy?" she asked softly. "Turn around and walk out those doors. Now."

"Ah, Kate, that hard expression of resolution ill becomes those lovely features. Let's see a bit of a smile turn up the corners of your pretty mouth, now that's a girl!" I extended my hands toward her and smiled idiotically. Instinctively she took a short step backward as she raised the evening purse waist-high.

"I'm warning you, Paddy!" she whispered harshly.

The mustached tycoon, who was now directly alongside

her, brought his hand down with surprising swiftness upon the velvet evening bag. There was a muffled explosion that seemed to stop the passage of time, freezing us into immobility for an endless moment no longer than a heartbeat. Then, as Kate twisted furiously to escape the grip of the mustached man, Stanley Beeson whipped out a slung shot from the waistband of his trousers and drew back his arm. Before he could bring the weapon into play, however, his arm was pinioned by the man who had worn the self-satisfied expression, who grunted, "None of that, now, laddybuck," as he twisted the "life preserver" from Beeson's grip.

The mustached man drew the now-empty derringer from the evening purse and slipped it into an inside coat pocket. My eyes followed his as he glanced down at the new hole in the rug, as large as a twenty-dollar gold piece. "Kate Linnett," I heard him say, "you are under arrest for the murder of Gus Gibbons and the attempted murder of Paddy Moretti."

Kate raised her chin, pulled back her shoulders and arched her back. Her fine breasts pressed as eagerly against the green watered satin as puppies against a pet store window. "Prove it," she said.

The mustached man, whose name was Lieutenant Donaher, ordered his two male and one female assistants to take the prisoners away "before the manager has kittens on the rug." I watched as the plainclothes officers led Kate and Beeson across the lobby. Just before Kate stepped out onto the sidewalk, she turned her head and called to me over her shoulder, "This isn't goodbye, Paddy Moretti—don't think so for a moment. It's just *au revoir*."

For a moment our eyes locked. I opened my mouth to answer, but found I had nothing to say. Then she was gone, and the door closed behind her.

Lieutenant Donaher put his hand on my shoulder. "It's

a good stiff drink you need right now, I'm thinking. Then you can come down to Centre Street and give us your statement, Paddy.''

"You're not going to believe this, Lieutenant, but I don't think I need a drink at all," I answered. "Now how do you like them apples?"

They didn't convict Kate of murder, or course. Nor even of attempted murder. Since most of the $120,000 worth of bonds was found in her room, the jury might have been able to persuade itself that she knew something about a bunco scheme, except that Mrs. Fowler refused to sign a complaint against her. The only thing she was found guilty of was discharging a concealed firearm in Sherry's Restaurant, and she drew a suspended sentence for that. (Stanley Beeson, however, was found to be wanted in three states, one of which immediately incarcerated him.)

The day she was released from jail I happened to be in New York City. Hochmuth mentioned the fact to me. "Your friend Lucrezia Borgia is tripping the city streets again, Moretti. Does that suggest a follow-up item to your incisive reporter's mind?"

I looked into his unappetizing face and frowned thoughtfully. "It's something a man would have to think about, Mr. Hochmuth," I answered.

I thought about it. Two hours later I was still thinking about it—it and Kate and Ike Murphy and Gus Gibbons and the Prince of Ixtapalapa and the whole snarled skein of duplicity and greed.

I bellied up to the bar in McSorley's. Old John decided to take my order, and raised his bushy white eyebrows inquiringly. "John, did you happen to know Taffy the Welshman?" I asked him.

"Taffy the Welshman? You mean Hugh Llewellyn, used to be with the Pinkertons? Yeah, I know him. How is he?"

"He's dead, John. He died in Saratoga this summer. Of drinking a glass of Irish whiskey."

"You don't say." John gave his head a single memorial shake. "He was a good man, Taffy was. He had a fine tenor voice." He wiped his bar-rag in a perfunctory half-circle on the bar. "What'll you have, Paddy?"

"Ale—two steins, John."

"Two steins, Paddy?"

"Yeah—the other one's Taffy's."

He nodded and drew two steins of ale. They understand things like that at McSorley's.

Author's Note

The black jockey Isaac Burns Murphy was one of the greatest winners in American turf history. He won 628 races in 1412 starts, including three Kentucky Derbies, four American Derby wins (run at Chicago), and five Latonia Derbies; his record of winning three principal races in one week at Churchill Downs—the Derby, the Kentucky Oaks and the Clark Stakes—still stands.

The only scandal of his career occurred in 1890, when, riding a horse called Firenzi, he performed so ineptly that many witnesses questioned his sobriety. Though Murphy was fond of champagne, this was the only instance of any such accusation against him. Murphy himself declared that he had been drugged by drinking some soda water that had been tampered with. Although the truth will never be known, I prefer to base my fictional episode on his version.

He was born in 1861 on the Fayette County, Kentucky, farm of David Tanner and developed his skills at the Fleetwood Stables of J.W. Hunt Reynolds. From 1884 to 1892, he rode for most of the prominent owners of the day and, in 1885, aboard James Ben Ali Haggin's *Salvador*, triumphed in one of the great match races in American history. *The Thoroughbred Record* remarked of him that he was "the nearest perfect jockey ever seen on the American racetrack. His judgment of pace was proverbial and his hand and seat defied criticism . . . His honesty was unimpeachable."

Through the efforts of the late Frank B. Borries, Murphy's

body was re-interred at Man o' War Park in 1967, with Eddie Arcaro presiding.

I am deeply indebted to Betty Borries for the voluminous research she has done on Murphy and on the racing scene at Saratoga Springs during the 1880s. Without her help, I doubt if this book would have been written.

For those who want to pursue the history of Saratoga Springs, the best book I know, and one I consulted often, is *Saratoga: Saga of an Impious Era*, by George Waller. Other resources I found valuable are *History of Thoroughbred Racing*, by W. H. P. Robertson; *The Remarkable Mr. Jerome*, by Anita Leslie; *This Was Racing*, by Joseph Palmer; *Giants of the Turf*, by Dan Bowmar III; *Famous American Jockeys*, by "Vigilant" (Walter Spencer Bosburgh); and *Turf Dictionary*, compiled by Earle Martin.

The Spirit of the Times (subtitled "A Chronicle of the Turf, Field Sports, Aquatics, Agriculture and the Stage") was an actual publication, and a lively one, published during the late nineteenth and early twentieth centuries, although, as far as I know, nobody named Moretti or Hochmuth was on its payroll.

Finally, be warned: Old con games, like old soldiers, never die—but unlike old soldiers, they don't even fade away. The Spanish Prisoner, newspaper reports confirm, is alive and well and enriching its practitioners in the United States today.

J.S.

About the Author

JAMES SHERBURNE, a well-known historical novelist, has turned to mysteries with the acclaimed Paddy Moretti series, the first two volumes of which became Detective Book Club selections. He lives in Midway, Kentucky.